Generation Snow

Robert Wildwood

To the Future of Life on Earth.

1

There was no more winter. Not winter as it had been known. Even on top of the tallest mountain there was no snow. A manufactured ice cube was ephemeral gold. The most exotic and expensive cocktails in the world listed ice as their first ingredient. People in poor regions of the South built shacks using skis and ski poles, scarves, snow shoes, snow boards, and multi colored plastic sleds for roofs. During the day climate refugees huddled inside for shade from the unregulated sun.

Certain herbs have a cooling effect on the body. Old Duffy had a special recipe for Peppermint Hibiscus Ginger Sun Tea that settled out all the guests of the Far North Cafe, and for those who could pay, you could get it with ice.

Duffy had been an owner in the Cafe Circle for seven years, after spending a good ten years of his youth rambling around the South working in solar radiation management, mostly painting roofs white in a desperate government program to reflect heat back into space. Duffy was able to save enuf money to buy into the cafe circle in the exclusive northern city of New Bear located on the new coastline of what used to be called Thunder Bay in Canada but was now called New World Gulf. Duffy was among a large percentage of the population that came from the South, as it was in many of the new high density Northern cities, many wealthy former citizens of the old United States moved North to escape the chaos. The United Tribes welcomed their resources to protect from invasion what had become some of the last livable lands on Earth.

There was plenty of excitement in New Bear with the diverse patronage of the Far North Cafe and the ever growing refugee crisis brewing in the South, people watching was always ripe. Duffy had learned to spot an illegal from the former United States, usually looking undernourished and overly tanned from weeks of rough foot travel under scorching sun, lacking quality possessions and clothing, extremely humble in demeanor, soft spoken, and if nothing else gave their status away often taking one sip of Duffy's herbal tea their body would quiver and convulse as the skin popped with goose bumps and muscles would spasm in the neck causing the head to lurch, all from the unexpected zing in the chilled beverage from a person normally accustomed to a single cup of warm puddle water per day.

Duffy noticed a well tanned man in the corner, a decent looking pack next to him probably filled with nothing but empty water bottles and some dried fish from the shrunken lake Gitchi Gami far to the South. To make it this far the illegal must be proficient at collecting wild edibles along the trail and stowing away on cargo transports, train or truck, even ships? Skinny little guy like that could fit in a lot of spaces. Unlike Duffy, who was a thicker, larger, darker man. There was something in Duffy's Brazilian, Native American, Norwegian genes that made him look very different from than this man in the corner, but being scared and alone, that was something Duffy could relate to.

Duffy stepped thru the kitchen and out back to a summer day in time to see a large raven pull a worm from the grass and look him in the eye before flying to the top of a blue spruce tree with it's beaked catch. Old Canada's Northern shoreline was now a waterfront paradise like those formerly found in the tropical south, a body of warm ocean water with a micro climate where phyto plankton still functioned, the food chain in the ocean had migrated and adapted and not yet collapsed as it had in the greater Atlantic and Pacific. Around the shoreline of this vast Gulf the United Tribes built high density housing for themselves, for some refugee tribes from the south, and for extremely wealthy patrons who were mostly white.

Duffy smiled looking on his fertile garden growing at the base of the gray concrete monolith that formed the walls of the cafe and the housing units above. Sea level rise had peaked when he was a child, now this place was safe from that fate for the long haul. If the climate was brought under human control, as scientists were attempting, and ice returned, the beach might travel away from the city of New Bear and beach front tourism could be lost, but that seemed a far distant future.

Duffy strolled to the greenhouse garden with it's protective roof, a shield against fallout from the melt down of the Pacific rim power plants, and harvested a grip of carrots which he took to the kitchen for cleaning. Duffy carved a carrot and plated it for the lonesome guest in the corner. The man looked up from his focus on the half empty glass of herbal tea and eyes widened to see the orange root on the brown glazed ceramic plate.

"Lovely," the man said. "I fear to know the price. How much?"

"On the house." Duffy said, "Greenhouse safe certified. Looks like you could use a fresh vegetable and I have plenty of carrots. As they say over on New Africa Island in the spirit of Ubuntu: I am because you are. "

"Miigwech."

"Miigwech."

"I grew up in the south, worked there doing solar radiation management. You're from there?"

"Not too far South." the man said.

"I wasn't accusing you of being a Floridian Pirate! There's no shame. Most of us in New Bear are in tribes from the South. Even the indigenous tribes here had a hard time surviving the total loss of cultural ways when the ice left, it was harder on them than it was on us. We had gotten accustomed to moving."

Duffy returned to the kitchen, there was prep work to be done before the wind mill workers came off shift in the afternoon when the winds picked up, they would be wanting a late lunch with rounds of ginger tea. Duffy pulled the chef from his pocket and took an update reading from the robo cook which sat in the middle of the kitchen like a large slumbering bear. Protruding from the top of the robo cook and giving it the look of an ancient church organ was a large assortment of variously sized transparent tubes filled with variously colored liquids, some completely empty with only residue lining the curved sides. Duffy reached up and removed some of these empty tubes while carefully reading the display on the Chef in his hand. He took the empty cylinders and entered the walk-in cooler to place them in transport containers, then pulled fully loaded tubes two at a time from transport racks and walked those out to the robo cook to install them with a quick push and counterclockwise twist. Soon the chef in his pocket buzzed three times and flashed green, the prep work was done.

Duffy programmed the evening's menu into the chef as he sat sipping an herbal tea in the dining room at his favorite table by the window overlooking the boardwalk leading down to the bay. The sun shone on the wind blown waves that rolled South to gently rock the floating fish pens anchored over deep water before running into the shallows and cresting in rolling foam on the jagged rock and log lined beach, a baby shoreline only decades old. The shadows of tall concrete housing blocks lay over the beach, confidently built in the knowledge that there was no more ice to be melted in the world. The high density housing blocks encircled the shoreline and stretched into the distance, on the ground floor of each one Duffy knew, a cafe just like his own Far

North Cafe. Each housing block or sometimes several levels in each block, were different according to overlapping multi cultural communities. There was New Shanghai, Little Mexico, Puerto Rican Heights, Cuba Town, Bali Block, and Maldivesville. Small communities forming the greater city of New Bear. All the cafes of the New World Bay were collectively owned and operated, members in the Cafe Circle, and once a week they gathered at a different cafe on a rotating schedule to discuss business practices: menu selections, robo cook service issues, food safety with radioactive contaminant detection devices.

Duffy's cafe was one of the oldest cafes in the greater circle, he took over it's operation from a woman who left to join the entertainment circuit, a life of travel, constantly meeting new people, and expectations of high energy nightly performances. Duffy sipped on fragrant tea, pursed his lips and shook his head once at the thot of such demands. It must be more work than play, all this rambling and rocking lifestyle. Duffy preferred relaxed cello sessions with only one or two other musicians, perhaps a singer on wild nights, maybe a performance once every month. With being on the road touring, constantly trying to cheer up a sad humanity, when would a person have a moment to read a book or appreciate the birdsong in the bushes?

As Duffy looked out the window with a smile for the Chickadees, Finches, and Cardinals dancing around his seed feeder, two figures in black emerged from the pine woods by the shore. The two heavy walkers turned up the boardwalk towards the Far North Cafe. Duffy did not recognize them as regulars. He took his hand off the tea cup and cleared his throat as intuition spoke, it felt like an unpleasant moment was approaching. Duffy often had these short notice premonitions, usually very specific, but this one felt like a complicated mystery.

The doors of the Far North Cafe swung open and the figures in black strode forward, scanning the dining room as the weapons detector above the door scanned them back and sent warning to the chef which lay on Duffy's table, it began to buzz and spin in circles.

One of the figures approached Duffy, "Where is he?"

Duffy reached out and silenced the chef and saw with some surprise the man at the table in the corner was gone, only the empty plate and glass remained.

"Oh! And that is why we have folks pay first. I don't have the peripheral vision that I used to."

"You spoke with him?"

"The Far North Cafe is a hands off place, if the customers need something they ask the robo server for it. I leave them alone unless they set off an alarm. I've got my finances worked out, I don't have to chase after tips."

Silence passed between them as the second figure spoke to an unseen connection while scouring the cafe's dark corners with his eyes, even smelling the air with flared nostrils.

"Are you in pursuit, officer? Who are you looking for?"

"They've got him." the second officer said, "He ran out the back door of this place!"

"Absurd!" Duffy leaned back.

The first figure pointed at Duffy, "Your face has been logged. Report to tribal police headquarters in this precinct. You will be questioned under suspicion of aiding an illegal." the two men dashed thru the kitchen and out the back door before Duffy could consider a response. Duffy remained seated at his table, less relaxed now, and practicing his anger management breathing.

2

That evening Duffy took a good shot of Valerian and Chamomile tincture to relax and sunk into a strange sleep. As his breathing became slow and regular he experienced rapid spatial movement but felt no wind on his face while his body flew thru darkness towards an unfamiliar galaxy. Star clusters filled the horizon and then Duffy was inside them, rushing past shining orbs and gas clouds, directly towards a triple star system and then closing on a single blue planet. Falling thru the atmosphere Duffy felt endless layers of clouds and thickening atmosphere and then the sight of oceans and continents, closing on a wide valley and green tree tops, down between trees, slowing to land on a well packed dirt road where a sentient bipedal toad with a colorful backpack was cheerfully skipping along.

Duffy marveled at a song he heard in his ears, a jazzy tune played on the piano that seemed to be coming from the toads footsteps on the path. As Duffy flew spirit-like among them, he felt the names of everything and everyone on this planet manifest in his mind.

Pagnellopy the toad was hopping to school, passing toad Grandstar's garden where La Fie Kas the jumbo cat sunned themself out front. Toad Grandstar poked their head out from a cover of thick vines, waving and smiling to Pagnellopy.

Further on, passing Xippix the turtle's house with Hank the dog out front, Xippix emerged at a run and joined Pagnellopy skipping along the path.

"Good morning friend!" turtle Xippix said.

"Pleasant day to you Turtle!" toad Pagnellopy said, "Right on time, as usual."

"Are you fully prepared for the first day of school?"

"Toad no!"

Further on Pagnellopy and Xippix were joined by best turtle friend Wixha, and as they cruised along other toad and turtle youth filled the path. Duffy felt himself one of them, knowing them like old friends, but was invisible and had no voice.

The young toads and turtles left the path and stepped to the cobblestone streets of Heart City and soon were among the multiple domes of their middle school. Pagnellopy found a place next to best turtle friend Wixha in a large domed classroom made of old dark stone. As the students found places the lights dimmed and then turned off, a large metal bowl sounded a resonating tone and the class quieted, stars filled the ceiling and audio filled the chamber as the cosmology review began.

"Welcome to the first day of school. Please direct you attention upwards. Here is our Great Ocean Galaxy, nineteen spiral arms full of stars. These three stars are at the center of our solar system: Figg, Tigg, and Bigg. Orbiting these stars you see our planet, Gaeiou. It takes 1000 days for Gaeiou to circle the suns. It takes 80 hours for Gaeiou to make a full rotation, we call this a day."

Pagnellopy felt the gaze of nasty Toad Chartles and shifted sitting position so their eyes would not accidentally meet.

The lesson continued, "When our planet comes closest to the smaller sun, Figg, which orbits our larger stars Tigg & Bigg, this is our Long Summer, the warmest part of the year. When Figg is on the far side of Tigg & Bigg, this is the coldest part of the year. When Tigg & Figg are equidistant to Gaeiou, this is our Short Summer, and when Figg is halfway around Bigg, this is our Small Winter."

Wixha turned to Pagnellopy, "Do you have trouble picturing this in your mind?"

Pagnellopy leaned into Wixha, "Ya. It's twisty."

Pagnellopy felt a spit ball bounce off their head. Pagnellopy glanced towards Chartles who sat across the room and Chartles owned the act by scowling at Pagnellopy as the stars whirled above them. Pagnellopy focused on the cosmology review to avoid getting angry.

"Gaeiou has 8 seasons, four short and four long, as determined by the movement of the suns Figg, Tigg, & Bigg. We believe this cyclical warming and cooling was essential to the formation of life on our planet. Many animals mate during the short summer season and then gestate their young during the short fall and winter, giving birth in the long spring, with the Long Summer and

Long Fall to mature."

The professor's face emerged from the darkness, a slightly illuminated warty old toad head, "Now let us imagine: What might life be like on another planet? Could life form on another planet with only two suns, or even just one sun? What do you think?"

"Brrr!" Wixha said, "Too cold. What would happen when the sun was on the other side of the planet?"

"That side of the planet would be completely dark." the professor said.

Pagnellopy straightened up, "If the ground had sufficient thermal mass and if the atmosphere had a proper mix of gases it could be warm enuf."

Chartles flung an arm in the air, "A planet with one sun would be a ball of ice."

"Okay, very interesting theories." the professor said.

Chartles whispered loudly at Pagnellopy, "TURTLE LOVER!"

"Don't listen Pagnellopy." Wixha said, "Nasty little rich toad. Look at the skin, a weird color green for sure. They keep that toad locked in a box."

Pagnellopy tried to focus on the lesson but all toad could think of was the hatred radiating from Chartles.

During lunch break from classes Pagnellopy & Wixha went to eat their Shum-Shum Fly and sour grass casserole by the pond at the center of the school. The clean water had eight willow trees surrounding it and twelve boulders near the shore to lay on. There were many students there, toad and turtle alike. Pagnellopy thot they would be safe here in the crowd, but then Chartles strode up with a nasty toad friend behind and said quietly, "Turtle lover."

Turtle Wixha scowled hard and the two bully toads kept walking.

Later in the day Pagnellopy was in Gaeioulogy class along with Wixha and many other toads and turtles, unfortunately including Chartles.

Wixha whispered to Pagnellopy, "Chartles is in this class too!"

Pagnellopy frowned, "Dry the hide!"

The Gaeioulogy Teacher stretched long toad legs in front of the class and some students giggled, "Welcome to Gaeioulogy 37! Let me briefly review what you should already know so that if you have any questions about this you can ask them now, don't be shy on the first day of school! So here we are, orbiting a tri-star system on the seventh arm of the Great Ocean Galaxy, our planet Gaeiou."

Pagnellopy whispered to Wixha, "Oh my god, this teacher!"

Wixha spun their turtle head in a circle with attitude, "You have to expect this on the first day."

The Gaeioulogy Teacher gathered thots pacing before the class, "Toad & turtle People evolved on separate continents but have a common ancestor from 600 million years ago before plate tectonics separated the land masses. Both species are fresh water swimmers and didn't meet until the development of salt water boating technology. At first toads and turtles had terrible wars but soon reconciled and are now economically and socially interdependent. Toads and turtles even celebrate each others holidays."

The professor stepped up and stood very close to the seated students, now speaking more quietly, "Perhaps someday toads and turtles will also share an intimate psychic connection, like cats and birds do. The deep mind spirit quantum connection which can be seen with the eyes, manifesting as a luminescent ring around life forms."

The Gaeioulogy professor broke the silence with a laugh and turned off the hologram, as the lights came up Chartles belched and inflated toad throat sack grossly large, causing some students to laugh.

"When you eat your lunch, try not to swallow so much air, Chartles." the Gaeioulogy professor clapped dark green hands together, "Well. Enuf! Lets read the introduction from tomorrow's lesson to get you interested: Toad and Turtle Sexuality."

Chartles belched again, more laughter.

"Are you alright Chartles?" the Gaeioulogy Teacher said, "Do you need to go to the little pond? Please feel free to leave. Oh, here we have a volunteer to read. Pagnellopy."

Pagnellopy straightened up and leaned into the tablet.

When school was let out Pagnellopy & Wixha walked home down the long well packed dirt and gravel road. They happened upon Chartles and nameless toad bully friend loitering on a moss covered stone bridge which spanned Num Num Creek.

"I saw your school profile." Chartles taunted Pagnellopy, "You're a member of the Toad & Turtle Alliance. TURTLE LOVER!"

"Seriously?" turtle Wixha stepped to the front, "Toads and turtles have lived together for like, three hundred years."

Chartle's friend twitched, "That don't make it right."

Pagnellopy clenched their first, "You are out of touch with reality, Chartles! People who deny the reality of science must also believe that you can sew a pocket on upside down and it will still work. You trust in science all day long but you ignore it when it comes to something that you don't want to believe is true. The world is growing colder and it's due to our global food farming practices. The evidence is mountainous."

"Turtles are dragging us down with hard backed lies. Toads have to fight back!" Chartles folded lumpy dark green arms.

"NO TURTLE LOVERS!" the accomplice said.

Wixha withdrew their head into shell and charged at the two toads, triggering the jump reflex on both and they made an involuntarily leap into the air, landing far below with a splash in the creek, followed by cursing.

"Come on Pagnellopy. Those toads know about my snap now." Wixha clicked turtle jaw together making a snapping noise and the two trotted over the bridge and were away.

3

Duffy looked out the massive plate glass window three stories above the Lucky Lavender, a cafe in the collective system operated by a Two-Spirited friend named Jameson Domahni, a man of Irish, Italian, Mexican, Russian, East Indian, and Navajo ancestry who spent much of his profits on rent for the luxury apartment with a perfect view of sunrise over the gulf. Diverse in racial background, Jameson was more singular in his cultural embrace, focusing on experimental clarinet compositions and sharing delicate small batch liquors in very reasonable servings which would never lead to a hangover. Duffy enjoyed playing cello with Jameson at times, tho he would never perform this duo in public. The pairing was enjoyable to participate in as a musician, but esthetically he found the music to be frequently hideous.

Jameson handed Duffy a miniature fruit smoothie made from local berries which he held with only two fingers so it wouldn't disappear in his hand, "I knew someone who was called to report for arrest but the system experienced a glitch and he was dropped. They checked for warrants, nothing. Let me tell you, he didn't do anything to encourage a recovery attempt on the files!"

Duffy let the fruit slide down and at that moment felt a small spark of hope as his throat glands constricted under the potent berries, "Hmm. Let's check the system after breakfast."

"You have the cafe on automatic? Your server-bot is reliable?"

"Yes. If I drop it from Ultimate Politeness to Friendly, still very reliable service, but every few days it will loop into paradox and I'll get a complaint about rude behavior. No big deal, people usually think it's funny. Nobody expects a robot to have serious issues."

"Alright Duffy. Drink your coffee, eat your breakfast, and tell me about this dream!"

Duffy looked out the window. A group of geese flew North up the coast, a ship glinted on the watery horizon of New World Gulf, "Vivid. I can tell you all about toads and turtles and the planet they live on, but I know it wont feel real to you, it will only sound like a funny dream. In my mind, my waking mind right now, I feel like something vast has turned on. Like a feeling I might have had as a child, that dawning of the light in your mind when you realize how big the world is and how little of it you know. I think this other planet is a real place."

Jameson put his mug down, "Oh yes, yes. I've got you. There are many ways to conceptualize that. The first thing that comes to mind is Quantum Consciousness."

Duffy shrugged, "Sounds like a fancy luxury vehicle."

"Oh yes, the most fancy. Quantum Mechanics talks about the possibility of wave-particle duality. One possible outcome of this theory is that our consciousness might be continually uploaded to another field and could encounter or experience another consciousness or reality in a way that ignores barriers of space and time. Two particles acting in identical ways but not connected by any known laws of nature. That's my understanding of it."

Duffy blinked.

Jameson nodded, "Okay, so there's no way for me to know what happened to you in your mind. But the dreams could be a message, a transmission. You may have been chosen. That guy in your cafe might have had something to do with it, I mean why right when he shows up? Or, okay, the dreams could be a quiet part of your brain trying to contact a louder part of your brain and make it listen."

"Perhaps triggered by the fear of being convicted and sent out on a border crew?"

Jameson shook his head and sipped coffee from his ceramic mug, "If this dream was an external transmission, it might not have come from this dimension. You know? Something you cant even put into words, but maybe you could express it mathematically. Some kind of quantum jiggling thing. Good luck with that. I'm just a cafe owner like you, the Lucky Lavender is my expertise, I'm not a physicist. Perhaps a more realistic idea is that you are experiencing the emergence of a mental illness."

Duffy threw his free hand up in surrender, "I beg you for relief. Thanks for the help. I'm good now. "

"Keep me updated! Let's see what you dream up tonight. For

now, back to Earth. Let's check your record for live warrants."

Jameson pulled a screen from behind a couch cushion and languidly scrolled thru information. Soon he fixated on an item and read it quickly line for line.

Jameson handed the screen over, "Bad news. You're wanted. We gotta get you outta here. An affiliate of the cafe system is an obvious suspect to harbor a fugitive."

"A fugitive? How about I turn myself in because I'm innocent?"

Jameson scowled shaking his head, and raised his eyebrows, "You really are innocent. There's a line of educated people trying to come North and scrub toilets with their degrees, you shouldn't jump into anything without allies and backup. If you do, we may never see you again. Immigration quotas, one person deported, another gets in. You know it's true. I hope you know it's true. The system is corrupt. Think about it, is there anyone who wants you out?"

Duffy was silent.

"Okay." Jameson stood up, "Here's what we do: move you out to my buddy Starblaze Sturgeon's place, she has a little artist colony out in the forest West of here, people coming and going all the time, wearing all kinds of costumes, nobody will notice one more freak. You'll have time to research and gather allies."

"Just like that. Wrong place, wrong time. One minute working my ass off and the next out the door."

"This life is not to be trusted Duffy."

Duffy pulled the Chef from his pocket, "I can set the cafe on long term vacation. The service bot was just upgraded and I've got two weeks of specials already programmed in. I can't imagine this situation will take longer than that."

"Well. You cant take the Chef with you, they can trace it."

Duffy stood up and handed the device to Jameson who placed it in a charging dock on a dark walnut shelf, "I'll take care if anything goes wrong."

Duffy turned away and stood close to the window, he could see the Far North Cafe over the top of a neighboring housing block.

"Artists. Will I have to wear a funny hat?"

4

Jameson arranged for Duffy to sleep on his couch and retired to his bedroom. As Duffy closed his eyes and sunk into exhausted slumber he began to visualize walking thru a sunset silhouette forest. Deep red skies stretched out beyond the lush green growth below and long black shadows of tree trunks ran away from the setting suns. Here Duffy came upon an arbor made of stone, moss covered and very old, in the middle of a beautiful garden. Again Duffy knew the names and relations of all the beings present: Toad Pagnellopy's old Grandstar was there, tending to some young sprouts in pottery bowls on a log table. Pagnellopy was there next to La Fie Kas the orange and yellow striped jumbo cat. Dusk was Pagnellopy's favorite time to visit Toad Grandstar's garden palace, when the sky turned colors of passionate flame and all figures became sharp in this vibrant sideways light.

"Pagnellopy, have you seen my telescoping back scratcher?"

"I'll help you look, Grandstar." Pagnellopy hoped up on toad legs and bent under the potting table, "Here it is!"

"La Fie Kas was playing with it again." Grandstar rubbed a toad hand over the cat's head, the eyes of La Fie Kas were closed in cat bliss.

"Grandstar, do you think there's life on other planets?"

"We think the answer is yes, most of us who think about it. Life on a similar planet would even look similar to us since the laws of physics are the same almost everywhere."

"People from another planet might look like me?"

"Yes. But instead of FOUR eyes they might have SIX!"

"Rooowr!" La Fie Kas yawned and stretched and lay their chin on orange and yellow striped front paws.

Cobalt the bird arrived and settled on a Forevergreen tree limb that arched high over the garden palace. La Fie Kas & Cobalt met eyes and communed with golden halos around their heads, silently exchanging information about a blood rat in the neighborhood. La Fie Kas arose and jumped from the palace window with a golden glow around.

"Do you think there are blood rats on other planets?"

"Maybe on another planet the cats have eaten them all."

"If there were no blood rats, what would cats eat?"

"Salad!" Grandstar whipped forth a large leaf from a basket of vegetables and shook it at Pagnellopy.

"And rainbows? Would rainbows on another planet have the same colors?"

"Light is light, but maybe people on another planet could see more frequencies of color than we can, or the atmosphere might look blue instead of amber like here on Gaeiou." Grandstar then wondered, "Maybe they can see pollution in the air, if only we could see the atmospheric pollution of Gaeiou we would know it was making the world colder. Should I suggest that to Professor Klauwz? A set of holographic reality lenses to place on our eyes."

Grandstar stepped onto the porch, the sunset horizon still visible. "Soon the snow will come. Too early again."

"First comes the rain." Pagnellopy said.

"The forever falling rain."

"And then the snow."

"Forever."

Beyond the patio a line of clouds crept along the horizon. Duffy floated away, and outside the garden palace in a small clearing by the woods, Cobalt stood with wings folded on a rock wall and La Fie Kas sat upright on the ground, ears rotating, listening to the wind. A muted golden aura undulated around the heads of the bird and cat, and as Duffy floated by in spirit their eyes followed him and Duffy felt a chill blow over his skin. On the ground nearby lay the half eaten carcass of a blood rat.

5

Starblaze Sturgeon was a Two-Spirit being. When she was born her parents called her a boy, when she could speak she explained to them she was a boy only a little and was fully a girl in many other ways so she would accept both roles when useful but would be called she and would present herself to the world as feminine, but if the day came when another woman asked to have Starblaze Sturgeon's baby, she could provide a second set of chromosomes. Her parents had no choice in this when a two-spirited being manifested so strongly in their child. Many years later they were happy that Starblaze required very little guidance, she was her own light. As a two-spirited being Starblaze Sturgeon crossed many boundaries without fear and saw deeper into the cosmos than others more accustomed to a narrower vision. She frequently helped those whose light was much dimmer in the world, people whose flame had been stomped upon and squelched, less fortunate beings.

Tied to the door of her cabin in the woods were long brown sweet grass bundles and wreaths of mint which as you reached for the handle would embrace you in their scent, and there holding the house for a moment, mindful of more than simply moving from outside to inside, the sweet grass and mint called to you: this too is a place and time to be cherished, at the threshold, the in-between outside and inside has a beauty, and how often should one stop to smell the flowers? That depends on how many flowers you find.

Duffy did not find Starblaze Sturgeon in the cabin but asked a handsome young man in the garden where to look and he sent Duffy to the creek that ran down a steep ravine set with huge cracked boulders and jumbo pine trees. Duffy had been on the coast so long that it felt strange to be in such country, dense vegetation, hidden spaces, surprises over each hill and endless little creatures skitting about on the forest floor and flying from branch to branch. In a place like this, so intricate, Duffy could imagine his dream vision creatures, the cats that talked to birds while hunting the blood rats in the wilds outside the garden of the toad and turtle people.

As he walked down the ravine Duffy thot about his home in New Bear. The coast was so predictable in modern times, only the weather ever changed, but it suited Duffy, the cafe was complicated and populated enuf to challenge his human drives. "Jameson." Duffy said his name aloud. Was Jameson taking care of his cafe? What specials had he re-programmed in the Chef? Duffy's reputation would suffer if he was gone long, Jameson's favorite food was algae fried steak smothered in ground hog gravy. Nothing wrong with a hearty meal, but the clientele of the Far North Cafe were particular folk, and they liked consistency. Duffy's customers came to the cafe with certain needs and those needs must be met to complete the transaction and perpetuate

Duffy's mildly relaxed lifestyle. Also, Jameson was in the collective political group World Circle Food Service, but he was also a competitor. As much as the city of New Bear strove to eliminate abusive capitalist practices, sometimes it was hard to put a name on behavior. One called it exploitation, another called it go-get-em-gusto. Duffy stumbled on a rock near the edge of the ravine and vowed to stop thinking negative thots, the present moment summoned his attention with dangerous ledges and precipitous heights.

"Hello!" a voice called to Duffy from the creek and he turned to the sound.

"Starblaze Sturgeon?"

She stood brown skinned and barefoot in the flowing water of a creek wearing a summer dress and black hair tied up, a pair of black boots sat on a boulder, "Ya! You should try this. Cold water on the feet really wakes up the entire body, toe to head. Very stimulating. If the water is cold enuf the pain will release endorphins in the brain and you will feel good."

"Oh. I prefer a glass of wine."

"The palate must be awakened. Your eyes will be opened. I have some wine you can taste after. Take the shoes off!"

"I'll try anything at this point. I have recently become aware of the transitory nature of permanence." Duffy perched on a small boulder and removed his boots, then swung around and put his feet slowly into the water. "Wow." Duffy looked down at small fish swimming around his feet and nibbling on spots they found tasty, "It's too much!"

Starblaze Sturgeon moved next to him, "Keep breathing. Just breathe. It's painful, but you're not actually being hurt. If you don't want to be tormented by the pain you can change what the pain signal means to the mind. Well, I've been told that but I never tried because I think it feels just fine to experience certain kinds of pain. Cold, hot, tattoo, piercing, alcohol placed on a wound, a knife cut, a hand slap on the ass, all the right measure and circumstance."

"My name is Duffy."

"Okay."

"Jameson talked to you, yes? He imagined I could stay at the artist retreat for awhile. Is this possible?"

"Such things are not entirely up to me, there are eighteen people out here and we each have a vote, except for Clairote, she gets two votes because we really like the way she cooks and we want her to stay forever. If a few of them take a disliking to you it might go bad. You operate a robo cafe? I think a few here will enjoy trying to convince you to work a different kind of life. It's fun to have a few hot heads around. You never know what's going to pop out of their mouths. Make sure to attend the play tonight, that will make a good impression on them."

That evening a play was scheduled in the large bowl shaped theater near the headwaters of the creek. Duffy had little interest in performance art at the moment, but with a population of eighteen people it would definitely be noticed if he failed to attend. When the time arrived he took his seat on a grassy spot of the circular hill, down at the bottom a rustic round wooden stage lay and four tunnels ran out of the hill for actors to enter and exit. The lighting was hung invisibly in the branches of several large trees that anchored the top of the hill. The play had three people in it, leaving fifteen plus Duffy for the audience. Duffy did not see Starblaze Sturgeon in the audience, she must be among the actors on stage. He considered each of the audience members in turn, a diverse bunch. Many races, cultures, and styles seemed to be present, but with modern biological transitioning technology, gene therapy, surgical techniques, and synthetic mood drugs one could never be sure if what was seen on the surface also represented the truth on a deeper level. Did it matter if a choice was made later in life or if it was a gift of birth? Or curse. In some card games, if one is dealt a hand that is unfavorable you can give the cards back to the dealer and have another hand dealt, only forfeiting one turn. Choice, or acceptance of fate. There isn't much respect in the modern world for people who simply accept their fate. But then, if you were born white and changed your race to Native American just to be accepted to the tribe and benefit from the arrangement of the modern world, are you a cheat? The power of technology had advanced to be almost indistinguishable from the ancient concept of magic. One could not believe their own eyes, which Duffy found to be true in the present moment as the play progressed into fullness it became clear that the script was actually a biography of Duffy's own life. No coincidence he thot, yes, the longer it went on there could be no mistake about it.

"Outrageous!" Duffy said under his breath, "By changing the lead character's name to Dunkin they thot to avoid some sort of liability." Duffy continued watching, staying calm and practicing his anger management in case he were actually experiencing some kind of temporary mental illness which might soon pass. Duffy noticed some of the audience were now stealing glances in his direction, each with a hardly suppressed grin. At last the scene came to the Far North Cafe when the illegal immigrant was in Duffy's dining room, and the actor who portrayed the fugitive was Starblaze Sturgeon.

"This place is a madhouse." Duffy fumed but felt paralyzed and unable to flee, fixated on the retelling of his recent life events. What would happen when the story got to the present moment, would a great spotlight shine upon him in the audience, and a participatory theater begin?

"What horror is planned for me!" Duffy whispered without moving his lips.

The story took a turn from reality when Duffy's character ended in bed with the fugitive, the two fully engaged in wild sex which was very realistically portrayed by the actors. Duffy's face turned hot red and he stiffened. Someone in the audience erupted laughing and the rest followed, the spell was broken and Duffy jumped to his feet so fast that he was air born for a moment and when his feet touched the ground he fled up and over the bowl, out into the darkness of a star lit night, the trunks of tall trees looming over him as he ran until he could hear no voice or breath but his own and slumped down against the bulk of a pine to stare at the wilderness sky full of lights shining from the center of worlds. Duffy wished he could be on a planet orbiting one of those stars.

6

Duffy pulled out his pocket tent and flipped it in the air, with a snap the tent deployed and landed on the ground, ready to go. Soon he was cozy and warm inside, wrapped in a golden polymer blanket like a warm burrito, and went to sleep with a heavy sigh, alone in the woods, but suspecting he would not be alone for long.

Soft voices in his ears like a small creek flowing, then a smell like food rising from the night, and songs of small birds snapped him into the present moment as his vision traveled down the roots of the pine tree below his sleeping body and up thru the trunk and out the branches of the crown, propelled further into the cosmos by the waving leaves on the night wind.

Duffy stood at the edge of a toad & turtle picnic arranged on a sunny beach that ran along a large lake. Here on soft reed blankets Turtle Pweon & Turtle Olleg reclined on portable wicker lounge chairs, their young Star Turtle Xippix & Hank the Dog. Toad Pagnellopy and their Grandstar also relaxed on the reed blanket. A spread of food occupied the center and several colorful lanterns on poles circled the gathering. Down by the water a group of very young toads and turtles fished in the shallow water and chased insects thru the tall grass.

"Strange weather we have today." Turtle Pweon said, their old distinguished shell comfortably nestled in the chair.

"Fires in the south cloud the sky." Turtle Xippix said.

"Fires go wild in dead areas of the country," Pagnellopy's Grandstar said, "and flooding has increased in the wet areas. The longer cold season does not allow the grasses to come to maturity and trees are dying off, the dead forests become tinder boxes. The Litak Trees do not bloom well anymore."

"Winter is too long." Pagnellopy said.

"And wild cats go hungry because rat populations dwindle." Xippix said, "Rats head north following the Chittle Bugs which can no longer survive the extreme cold."

"We too may follow the Chittle Bugs North to escape the burning cold that has settled into the middle lands." Pagnellopy said.

"And our grand children have seen too little summer." Grandstar said, "At the end of Long Winter there is nothing left in the library to read. They miss swimming and stretching out on warm rocks in the summer, it was our ancient joy!"

"This again!" old Turtle Olleg spasmed in their folding wooden chair, "Trying to enjoy a picnic and always the radical politics come out. Once upon a time our people hibernated in the winter, under the mud. Now it is too cold, but we have technology, we can enjoy winter. Our species has developed mental illness from the lack of hibernation, it is true, but scientists are working on this. There are very hopeful medications being developed. This is serious, but the sky is not falling, we can engineer hibernation systems to serve our needs. We must simply face this truth and adapt to these new circumstances, that is all. The Gaeiou will bring itself back into balance. The creator did not make a flawed creation. We are strong! We will survive."

"No! We can stop this process." Grandstar clapped dark green toad hands, "We must restore the planet's energy balance & stabilize our climate. If we focus only on adaptation many species will die, possibly including toads and turtles."

"As a student scientist I know." Xippix said, "This concerns everyone on Gaeiou, but the long term vision is beyond the reach of our present moment's focus. People must be educated to fire the passion that is needed for us to restore the balance!"

Olleg guffawed and shook turtle head, "We cannot destroy the Gaeiou. We are not so grand of creatures. It's impossible."

"Many disagree. We see what happens to those in respected positions who speak up, they are branded alarmist and their funding is cut. Those who speak out become marginalized and are silenced. The remaining scientific community is afraid of destroying their careers and they remain silent. There is good money to be made in shutting up and destroying the planet."

Grandstar turned, "Xippix can tell us, courage is a virtue our scientists are not taught in school. We must stand beside them. This is too important and too urgent."

Olleg clucked in turtle's chair, "Toads & turtles have always claimed the sky is falling. The end of the world is always right around the corner. There's always something to be afraid of, that's just part of our evolution, making fight or flight decisions. But the sky never falls and people go on living and dealing with whatever hardships come their way."

"Back to the present moment." Turtle Pweon sitting next to Olleg fanned their turtle head with a Trinka Palm leaf, "Please! I am trying to relax here. I have birthed a thousand tadpoles and I'm sure I will a thousand more. Look over the lake, there goes a red winged Bortang Bird! Life goes on."

"There is a difference now." Grandstar said, "Claims of catastrophe in the past were not based on science. There is scientific evidence now from every branch of science that points to a single conclusion: the sky is not falling, it's filling with pollution produced by our farming activities and this is cooling the planet. This is no theory, it is happening as we sit here."

Olleg flourished a turtle hand, "So says toad science. Even if that is true, how would we feed our nation without the fish farms? Alternative agriculture is impractical and expensive. We are not all wealthy toads."

Xippix spoke quietly, "The true cost of our current system is predictable destruction. What could be more expensive than that?"

Olleg spoke loudly, "Reducing consumption is highly unpopular for us turtle People. The wars were harder on us. We are still rebuilding and progressing. Perhaps the toad people could stop eating so many fish so we turtle people could have our fair share."

"Reducing is not popular with toad people either." Grandstar said, "The toad nationalists want to grow a glorious civilization not stunt it before the final empirical bloom. We must deal with this as a planetary civilization, as citizens of Gaeiou. We share the same atmosphere, we must work together. Turtle and toad!" Grandstar held a fist to the sky as the Bortang Bird flew over them.

"World government?" Olleg recoiled and turtle's old wooden folding chair groaned and creaked dangerously, "The memorials to the wars between toad & turtle are still polished and honored with fresh flowers every spring. There is respect and trust between our people, but there is not enuf love for such a deep embrace. Even young turtles know you shouldn't trust a toad with your life. It's harsh but true. Tell me it's not the same in toad culture?"

"You are a stubborn old turtle!" Grandstar put toad hands on belly, "What's it take to get a fresh idea inside that shell? To rely on bureaucrats to draw out a treaty between our peoples is precious time that we should instead be spending on reducing the damage immediately. While leaders talk, Gaeiou is being ruined."

"The sky is falling! The sky is falling!" Ollege waved fingers in the air, "Look around, this lake, the trees, the grass and flowers, do you think we can destroy this even if we tried? The Gaeiou will come back into balance, we will adapt along with the Gaeiou. The creator is all around us. Enjoy your picnic, crazy old toad!"

"Yes! Enjoy this!" Pweon said, "Let's move off this nasty subject before the old green skins start dueling with their canes. What a lovely sunset is coming upon our outing. In the words of the poet Saucro: 'Red is the delight! Zesty Nastu flowers on the tongue zing fire up our noses! Crisp exoskeleton of lunch, bite of the Shum-Shum Fly our call to dinner. Deep ancient green the skin of my First Star, knock knock the beak of a Tartang on the shell of my Second Star, we turtle, and the delightful dance of the Tartang birds mating, we remember old times, we return to the country from where we hatched. Today is a beautiful day: let three suns radiate life and awaken our joy to send it singing from our shells and mouths.' "

"Today is a beautiful day." Olleg folded hands on turtle belly and smiled.

7

Duffy boarded the ferry to Nunavut Island along with the rest of the tourists and workers, using an ID set that Jameson provided him. Fugitive created by a fugitive, how often had this tragedy played out in human history? Duffy ran thru the details in his mind and lamented this ridiculous turn in his solid middle years, "Here I go rambling about like I was in my 30s again, ready to catch the next shuttle to anywhere that wasn't here." Duffy considered again the concept that this whole mess was actually a scheme by Jameson to gain possession of the Far North Cafe, a power grab within the collective. Jameson could have easily arranged the presence of an illegal immigrant in Duffy's dining room and then tipped off the tribal police, sent Duffy to the art colony in the forest just as extra fun. "They may have declared me missing and seized the Far North already, but what motivation could Jameson have? A person operating in the Cafe Circle can only own one cafe at a time."

Duffy ceased talking to himself and sunk into a window seat, watching the waves on New World Gulf he was rewarded by the sight of dolphins on a parallel course with the ferry lunging from the water in graceful arcs. On the horizon the sun was shining on the broad forests of New Africa Island with it's massive line of windmills on the water. Further on the ferry passed a group of fishing boats of the indigenous people from Qikiqbatu Island, setting out nets to see what mystery fish the changing climate had brought them. For thousands of years it was the same, a sustainable harvest but most of the cold loving creatures had been killed in the big die off. When there was nothing left to eat, would humans eat each other? Duffy shuddered, watching a pertinent news report on the wall, "-the Anthropocene Age continues, accelerating toward a non-existent conclusion while at the controls the greatest procrastinator ever known: humanity, waiting for the very last moment to turn away from the cliff and wondering if our eyes have played tricks on us, is our perception of progress actually our bodies falling thru the air because we have already jumped off the cliff and are halfway to the bottom?"

"Margarita sir?" Duffy rolled his head in the fabric covered deck chair to accept the sensibly stable wide bottomed cocktail glass from the bar bot.

"Miigwech."

"Miigwech."

Duffy sipped on the tasty drink and gave an extra moment of appreciation, thinking that perhaps there might be only a few hundred years more of cocktails before the manufacture of ice became impractical. "Dreadful prospects, humanity should go extinct before cold and zingy citrus beverages do. I wonder what beverages toads and turtles enjoy?"

A ship's horn sounded, deep and resonant across the sparkling water. The ferry responded in a tone an octave higher. Duffy watched the approaching ship come into view over the rim of his bev. A red freighter with white deck and six story pilot house in back with numerous black windows like eyes. Behind the thick nautical glass Duffy imagined invisible insect-like humans staring out of this strange floating hive of humanity. A ship transporting grain or concrete for a new high density housing complex? Wind generator parts? Rocket parts for the exploration of other worlds? If the last, Duffy supported the effort.

"Considering what humanity has done to Earth, we had best be working hard on a backup plan." Duffy sipped his cocktail.

Earth was a durable good, but there was only one for everyone to share, a hard situation for a durable good. Duffy thot about the heavy grease nipple on the main pump of his robo cook and shook his head, wondering if Jameson was paying proper attention to the daily diagnostic reports.

A loud siren call came from the ferry's mast, a noise such that one could not possibly ignore it, and then silence, and a voice: "Attention! Everyone below deck! Seal the hatches!" The message repeated as tho to convince children and true soon enuf all had gathered inside and closed the steel doors. All available windows were crowded with passengers.

"What is this?" Duffy demanded of the nearest person.

"Pirates!" the woman said, and clinked her glass with a smile on

Duffy's own margarita, "No worries, it's become common now. They usually look like little fishing boats and then next thing you know they're climbing ropes up to the deck and taking hostages then back down and zip they're gone again. Hostage fetches a decent price sometimes. I guess they really are fishermen, it puts food in their mouths. This one is different, a big one! Floridian Pirates maybe. There could be a whole city of people living on that ship. What a world." She sipped her drink and craned to look out the large plate glass window.

Bright flashes of light in the sky and the ferry they stood on shuddered in a shock wave.

"Dear mother!" Duffy sloshed his drink to the deck as he bent his knees to keep from falling, "The ticket master back in Belai failed to mention this possibility!"

The woman laughed at Duffy, "Don't you hear the news? Have you been living up a tree?"

"I am a humble businessman. The world is full of disturbing news which is not pleasant to discuss with customers, therefore I do not fill my head with it."

Another series of midair explosions sent flashes of light and then shock waves thru the ferry. The windows were now so crowded with spectators trying to get a better look that the bev-bots were having a difficult time navigating and completing transactions. A young girl accosted a confused bev-bot and stole a pink cocktail, slamming it down in four huge gulps.

The woman standing next to Duffy at the back of the crowd gestured with her glass, "I've never seen such a vigorous exchange! The pirates are usually very poorly armed."

A massive fireball rolled skyward from the red freighter and Duffy was sorry he had been looking directly at it, for now he could only see yellow circles as happens when one looks at the sun. The crowd began cursing in shock. The red freighter still surging towards them bore huge holes amidships and was sinking fast. Fire spread across the water as a ruptured tank spilled out. So close was the ship now that tiny flashes of movement could be seen jumping from the deck to the water. Duffy tapped a man looking out the window with binoculars, "May I?"

The man lowered the eye piece and handed it to Duffy, "I have seen enuf."

Duffy took his place at the window and scanned the ship, the entire deck of the freighter was filled with agitated people, mostly light skinned people, hundreds, a thousand, how many were still below deck? Duffy scanned the water around the sinking ship and thot to see the splashing of windblown waves, but each white cap of foam had human heads and arms. Some had small buckets they clung to, some small rafts, some hanging onto random debris, all were being mobbed by desperate swimmers who clung to the sides and pulled everything floating down.

Someone said, "How many can we pick up? It seems like our ferry is at capacity already." No one replied. The ferry pulled away rapidly from the sinking freighter which disappeared underwater.

"It is prophecy." a man turned from the window and spoke to the crowd, "The white man's world is rolling back, sinking under the ocean. What remains will be beautiful and green."

"This ship we stand on is the white man's ship," a gray haired woman spoke from the back, "and those drones we fly, the white man's technology. We use these things now, and how different are we from the white man when we use his ways? Here we are many colors even at this window, native tribes all survivors of genocide for hundreds of years, survivors of the African slave trade, and all of us survivors of Capitalism, but does our history make us righteous in all we choose to do? Now we have the sword, and what have we done? Put on the mantle and it weighs heavy, we have crowned ourselves god! The burden is too heavy."

A young man next to her spoke, "There are many prophecies, as many as we have people who dream in the spirit world. We must look back to our old ways and remember the wisdom there."

The gray haired woman spoke again, "We must remember and share the wisdom that has been shut away. Quiet and dark wisdom that is so hard to see and hear with all the bright lights and loud sounds. We can never go back, but also we cannot stay here in this place."

The engines of the ferry did not shift and slow to help survivors but continued at full speed until the scene was fully aft and in ten minutes the debris that remained floating was nothing but a small dot on the horizon.

8

Duffy lay in his warm bed with fresh cotton sheets at the Inn of Rainbow Lights on the most beautiful resort island in New World Gulf, his eyes wide open and wondering if he could ever sleep again. At last a gentle breeze blew and he found himself in a garden. It was toad Grandstar's garden palace, and Turtle Xippix was there with Turtle Wixha.

"This garden is beautiful." Wixha said, "You've done such good work here."

"Thank you." Grandstar said, "I have a lot of love for this place."

"Has the cold damaged anything?"

"Yes, the fruit trees, and some of the vines are gone. Some I can wrap in fabric and shield from the new harsh winters. I used to feel righteous about my little piece of the wild, the water wheel generator that provides my electricity and the tricycle I ride into town. I worked hard to live in a way that would not pollute the Gaeiou, but one person's lifestyle does not save the Gaeiou. We are all connected to the biosphere as a whole and not everyone is so privileged they can live this way. The fish from the feed farms are cheap and even tho it pollutes the atmosphere and is cooling the planet, those fish are all that many turtles and toads can afford."

Grandstar touched a nearby plant and a gold halo rose between toad & plant, "Life! Right there. All around us. It's free! The census recognizes me, a toad, and turtles, cats and dogs even, but not these plants! We should count the plants, they matter! They are everywhere, we call them weeds, and smaller bacteria, everywhere. Bacteria could survive the cold longer than anyone, some bacteria survive in frozen ice or a full boil. Life! Right here. Who are we to decide for Gaeiou what lives and dies? Maybe Olleg is correct, creation is perfect, if we destroy ourselves, life will continue. No more toads and turtles, but insects, bacteria, birds? Life will continue, but different, is this what nature wants? We have accelerated evolution."

"No more philosophy, Grandstar. It is time for us to take responsibility for our planet." Xippix said, "We that are alive are collectively the brain of this world. We can understand and act."

Wixha clicked their turtle hands together, "How can we possibly teach these concepts to enuf people in the short time we have? And how can we stop turtle lands from polluting, we have no control over turtle government. We have to do something! We have to make them stop."

Grandstar sat on a moss covered stone bench, "The Holding Ponds are full of toads and turtles who have already tried that. There is blood on the hands of the righteous, and we ask ourselves, are they still righteous? Our governments call them terrorists and dismiss their moral motivation. What seemed like the righteous way was a failure, except that it may have inspired people to keep trying other ways. Now we must reach out and organize not as toads and turtles but as the collective Citizens of Planet Gaeiou. I am old and know there is no time to waste. I do care about what the future thinks of me.

"How do we do it?" Wixha said.

"How DO we do it?" Grandstar said.

"If an old toad will trust a young turtle, I have ideas." Xippix said, "Organize global alternative food production coalitions. We can use our communications buttons and amplify the psychic connection that all life on Gaeiou shares, project holograms of toad & turtle circles from all across the world. Thirty three percent will equal critical mass and society will roll over."

"You seem very confident! The future is yours." Grandstar held out toad hand, "I like your idea. If people stopped using the factory farms to produce our food and did it another way, then the alternative food wouldn't be alternative anymore, it would just be how we get our food. I will help any way I can, and if they throw me in the hole with the rest of the toads, so be it. I have lived a long life. "

"We need a push." Wixha pumped a turtle fist.

"A big push." Xippix said.

"Let's push hard." Wixha pumped both fists.

Pagnellopy entered the garden palace from the front path, "The

meeting is at 16, meet at the old council circle in the North woods.
I think it will be a good turnout."

"Let's pick some fruit from the garden to share." Grandstar said,
"We have a lot of work to do."

9

Duffy woke up feeling angry, it was unreasonable. Here he was on the finest resort island in the nation of Nunavut, forced to vacation on the ocean shores of a warm Northern rainforest, wooden boardwalks and fiber-formed cabins floating on jumbo buoyancy chambers anchored in sheltered coves, fully prepared for hurricane or other wild weather patterns with waterproof cabins and weather alert systems. Even a tsunami would only sweep the resort around a bit, so the brochures claimed, like a fish hooked on a line. Here Duffy could lounge under a thatched canopy on an easy recliner while the hot summer rains fell. Why the feeling of anger? He missed his cafe, his regulars, it was a bit lonely here. This was costing him too, the credits were going down, hard to relax knowing how much it was costing, even with Jameson paying for half. And why was he paying? Odd. Were they truly such good of friends? Duffy couldn't recall the last time he was able to attend Jameson's birthday, always so much to do at the cafe.

Anger at the suffering of the boat people. The freighter and all hands. A massacre, yes, much different to experience in person. News reports were graphic but did not convey the entire feeling of such an experience. Being in the presence of thousands dying had a serious consequence on the emotions.

World wide the population crash continued. A body count

showed up in the daily news, steadily counting, meaningless numbers, billions dead now. A certain number of people died every day, Duffy grew up knowing that. The faces he had seen in the binoculars now flashed in his mind as he listened to news of the refugee crisis, faces like those of his customers, real people.

Duffy's phone buzzed, it was Jameson sending word that the situation with Duffy's warrant was nearly resolved, actual good news. By the time he returned to New Bear it might be done. Duffy resolved and booked the journey immediately, by boat and train, he would leave tomorrow, and looked out on the water which rolled in short waves lapping against the wooden bulkhead of the floating dock, a rare southern wind brought by a hurricane raging far up the Mississippi River which in old times had been a delta that bore the brunt of storms but now with peak sea level rise the water was a massive inlet that reached deep into the Midwest and granted hurricanes water front access to such places as Arkansas and Tennessee.

Four generations back Jameson's Irish ancestor forever changed the fortunes of his family by joining a Northern tribe thru marriage. A hundred years of racist hatred for mixed blood folk, now paid off, they were of the chosen people in possession of some of the last habitable lands on Earth. An incredible change of fortune, hard fought and won. There were whole island nations living on old cargo ships, farming vegetables on the decks, de-salinating water with solar power, surviving, anchored in harbors of friendly nations but not quite allowed citizenship. Permanent boat people from drowned coastal cities across the world.

Duffy's own family escaped the fate of all Southerners in a similar way to Jameson's family, his parents had just the fraction of native genes to be included, and they suffered such judgment at being more white that native that when racial transition surgery became viable at the turn of the century they offered to pay for Duffy to become half genetic Ojibway and, as a pre-teen, he agreed after reading several scientific studies which concluded that racism, at it's present diminishing rate, was not going to be eliminated from human culture for another 3600 years, well beyond Duffy's projected life span. It was easier to perform on a person when they were young, prepubescent. The procedure to alter racial appearance was made illegal in the North when it became common for illegal immigrants to undergo the change to successfully flee into the North. For this reason, and because prejudice still existed, Duffy never told people about his decision. Mostly Duffy did not feel like a mixed race, he felt like a whole himself living in a mixed up world.

Duffy respected the elders, the traditionalists. A lot of people he knew didn't care about the old ways. Duffy felt like an Indian, it was one of the cultures he grew up in. Sometimes he looked at a mirror and imagined being only one race. White, European, what was that like? To be a stranger on foreign soil, illegal. Duffy wondered if it would have been brave to stay the way he had been born, fight to exist in his lighter skin, to be hated and loved differently simply because of his skin. "No regrets." he often said aloud to himself, and thirty years later he sometimes still found himself saying those words. Life was clearly much more enjoyable than being hated by everyone for not being solidly on one side or the other. Whenever Duffy saw a person of new race on the street he was always extra kind to them, thinking they couldn't afford any transition, but sometimes he wondered if some people might actually choose that inbetween world and tough it out.

"Duffy!" his name rang out over the water and bounced off the wood deck and into his ears like a crack of thunder and he bounced involuntarily in his lounge chair. Starblaze Sturgeon stood at his blind side smiling, knowing she had surprised him.

10

Duffy sprang to his feet and dashed away, glancing behind only as he reached his floating bungalow, making sure no one saw him enter. There he stayed until darkness fell, packing his few belongings. He caught sight of himself in the full length mirror, he wasn't thin but felt thin, empty, alone, like the man sitting in his cafe a short week ago.

"Why would Starblaze be here?" Still suspicious Duffy slipped his head out the bungalow door and saw no face but the waning moon rising over the hills to the east. Duffy went for a walk to clear his head, "Perhaps I should loosen my grip on this grudge. Thespians will be thespians. Cultural tricksters! I was the one who sought them out. Should I have felt honored to be artistically skewered in the play?"

Arriving at the bungalow hub an illuminated poster on a kiosk caught his eye, a colorful image of Starblaze Sturgeon in costume for a play that would be performed in the great hall at the resort that very evening. "Question answered." Duffy said aloud, and contemplated the situation: "If I hadn't booked tickets away I would certainly attend. Starblaze is a passionate performer who should be supported even if the participant is discomforted. I've been unable to appreciate her work from a perspective of self involvement that has narrowed my vision to a point where I now suspect I might not know what's really happening anymore. A broader vision is necessary, and clearly that is the goal of the art."

Duffy strolled back under the subtle illumination of the moon on the rippling gulf waters. He resolved to delay his travel, if possible, and take in this play. From the poster it seemed this piece was not based on his life and so might be more enjoyable anyway. Duffy did not like making enemies and it seemed his departure from he artist colony might have disappointed some potential customers. Being in the customer service industry required paying attention to whom one gave the middle finger to.

Arriving at the door to his bungalow he stopped, the windows were dark but a light inside flashed back and forth as tho searching, someone was in his room!

11

Out of shadow dark green faces emerged, eyes among the forest leaves and hidden behind trunks of Forevergreen trees, the buzz of Shum-Shum flies thick in the bush. Turtles and toads crouched silent in the grass and underbrush of a woods near the industrial track that lead to the main chemical plant outside Heart City. Green skin was camouflaged by green leaves, like in the old days, no one wore the brightly colored and sparkling fashion that was now common, stripped down they waited. The lights of a sulfide train shone down the tracks and soon lumbered past. The group emerged like a swarm, toads riding on turtle backs, toads hopping from turtle backs up into the gondolas and throwing rope down for the turtles to climb. Pagnellopy, Xippix, Grandstar, Wixha, Xippix's dog Hank running alongside, many other toads & turtles rode the loaded train into the processing plant. Once the light of the suns was blocked by the roof of the plant they jumped from the train and began their tasks.

"To the tower!" Grandstar led the way to the central core, opening the elevator they all loaded in, the doors slid shut and the car jolted, the ride took an excruciating amount of time to reach the top, passing by every floor they looked out the window at the factory workers going about their jobs.

The doors to the elevator opened and they dashed forward, down a long hall and into the control room, the workers were surprised and then overwhelmed, "No more work today." Pagnellopy said, "Be safe and go home." Their toad and turtle companions led the workers to the elevator and Wixha locked the doors.

Grandstar leaned over the control panel, "And now let's see how thorough my research has been. Come on you old engineering degree! In my youth, we didn't talk to our friends using buttons on our coats, we talked thru a box that sat on the table and it stayed in the house! But that's why we have a brain, am I right, to keep learning."

"Grandstar's got it!" Pagnellopy shouted.

Xippix looked down from the window. Grandstar pushed buttons and slid fingers across the smooth surface. Xippix opened the window and set up a multi projector hanging outside, the words appeared written with light on the tall control tower of the plant, "ALTERNATIVES NOW!"

Grandstar handed a button to Pagnellopy, "Let's begin live communicating immediately. We can use the control room backup batteries for now, they can't shut those down from outside."

"Citizens of Heart City and all of Gaeiou! This is the citizen occupied Bio Feed Plant. We are shutting it down. No more pollution in the atmosphere. Please stand in solidarity and help us immediately transfer to renewable food sources and meanwhile reduce consumption as much as possible. This cannot happen overnight-"

A loud voice called from the ground outside the tower, "Xippix! We know you are up there!" it was Olleg, Xippix's Second Star, "Come down before you get in real trouble!"

"Xippix! Xippix!" Pweon, called up, "I am your First Star. I will always be your First Star. I would be your happy First Star if you came down here now."

Xippix stared down at the ground far below, "God. It's my Stars, and a bunch of riot toads behind them. How did they get here so quick? Somebody tipped them off." Xippix shouted out the window, "Join us! We all live under the same sky!" Xippix turned inside, "Pagnellopy. You better come see this."

"My Stars." Pagnellopy said, "They're gonna jump right up into this window, that's how mad."

Pagnellopy's First Star standing with Olleg and Pweon shouted up, "You come down out of there! Is this how we raised you? No!"

Grandstar put a head out the window, "We might not raise our children the right way the first time, but it's never too late."

Pagnellopy's First Star jumped in rage halfway up to the window, face expanding in size and at the top of the jump yelled, "Unbelievable!"

Pagnellopy and Xippix jumped back involuntarily.

"Your classmate alerted us to this plot," Pagnellopy's First Star shouted, "Unfortunately too late to stop it. Come down immediately!"

"Who ratted- Chartles?" Pagnellopy said, "Must have overheard us. At least Chartles bungled the snitching somehow so that we had enuf time to get in."

Pagnellopy's Second Star held their arms out, "Pagnellopy! Is anyone hurt? Are you alright?"

"Everyone is safe. For now. Let's talk about the future: no, we're not safe. That's why we're here. If you believe it's true then you've got to speak up and support what we're doing."

Pagnellopy's Second Star pointed a finger like a tool, "There's a camera crew at the front gate. I'll go talk to them right now!"

"What!?" Pagnellopy's First Star turned away from the tower and watched toad's Second Star strut towards the gate, long fine fabric of their garment flowing out behind them.

A loud barking came from inside the control tower, Xippix's dog Hank barking repeatedly with hackles up and facing down the long hallway. Xippix and Pagnellopy rushed down the hall and peeked out the doors and saw something dreadful: Wixha talking to toad riot police who were slowly and quietly filling the hallway from a stairwell next to the elevator. Hank the Dog nosed open the door and charged out at the gathering police, Xippix screamed his name. The police took aim and sprayed stink gas at Hank which caused the small dog to express defense glands all over the police and Wixha. Horrible cries echoed in the hall as Hank ran back to the control room and Pagnellopy slammed the door while Xippix keyed the lock. Grandstar stepped between the gasping and drooling toad and turtle to attach an encrypted magnetic bolt to the door.

"They cant get in!" Grandstar said, helping Pagnellopy back to the control room.

Xippix was pouring water from burning turtle eyes and gasping for breath, "A traitor!"

Pagnellopy had clenched fists, "We lost the elevator and stairs, no way in or out now but the windows and the roof. I cant believe it. They almost got us."

"Are you alright?" Grandstar coughed, "God! I have been alive a long time, but that is the worst smell I have ever experienced."

Pagnellopy put one hand on the wall, "My legs are twitching like I might accidentally jump and brain myself on the ceiling."

Grandstar held Pagnellopy in toad arms, "I've got you, just breathe in, breathe out, let your legs go limp, relax."

Xippix was gagging now partly on the pain compliance mist but mostly on the glandular expression, "I wish I could crawl up into my shell. I can't believe that smell came out of Hank. Let's open all the windows. Hank are you alright?"

Hank sat huddled under the control room desk shaking. Xippix rummaged in a duffel bag and produced a spray that he used on the entire room, then on Hank, "If it works for police stink gas it might work on glandular secretions too." It was true, soon the noxious odors had been chemically neutralized.

"The transmitter is online." tho liquid rolled from all four of Grandstar's eyes who showed no other sign of distress and flashed a smile, "I'm going to start casting while you three recover. There's a few perks to aging and a dulling of the perceptual senses is one. I put stronger spice than that on my breakfast."

Grandstar activated the button and a golden halo encircled toad head and surrounded the broadcast equipment, "Citizens of Gaeiou! We speak to you from the solidarity of three living generations who want there to be many more to come. We are causing the climate of Gaeiou to change, the falling temperatures must be stopped. Our actions today are not the end, we know the infrastructure cannot be changed in a few days. We have performed this action today to reach those who still do not understand that something must be done, and to inspire those who already know in their hearts. The time of doing nothing is over. Rise up toads and turtles! Our generation will not be the last! Rise up for those suffering in the drought lands! Rise up for those hungry in the small towns whose crops have failed! Rise up for those who are now homeless and do not have enuf food to eat and who's very feet have been frost bitten and amputated from the extreme cold, rise up for the old ones who have lost their minds during the Long Cold Winters that are longer than ever in recorded history. Remember their stories of the glorious summers,

we want those back! We call for all workers in Bio Feed Factories
to rise and join with other workers in non-polluting food
production and give birth to a new structure. There are other
ways of living, we must compel the old ways to end so that new
ways can be born. Actions must continue on all continents. Shut it
down and start it up! Bring the balance back!"

Below the control tower a wild scene erupted. Many young
toads and turtles were being sprayed by the police and drug away
in nets. A line of ambulances arrived and some toad police were
being treated by medics wearing breathing apparatus, and further
out, beyond the security fence hundreds of supporters gathered,
held back by lines of riot toads.

Nightfall brought a slight quieting to the plant. Lights of the
plant snapped on, illuminating the solidarity camp out by the
front gate. Then the lights went out, all of them, and the crowd
cheered, and a broadcast came thru Grandstar's button and into
the public address system of the plant, "The workers of the power
industry stand in solidarity with the occupation of the Bio Feed
Plant! Only power for hospitals and essential services." The crowd
roared and jumped. In the distance, the tall buildings of Heart
City lay dark, shapes outlined by the stars in the sky.

Small camp fires sprang up by the front gate and the evening
calmed considerably. Grandstar sat by the tower window
watching and contemplating the sky, Pagnellopy by their side.

"We don't usually see so many stars this close to the city, do we." Grandstar said, "What if it was always like this? City buildings dark late at night, we could see the stars! What a beautiful vision."

Pagnellopy looked out on the sky: "It would save energy too. Oh Grandstar, half our crew is rotting in the Holding Ponds now. Have we done the right thing? It feels like things won't ever be the same."

Grandstar breathed in and out, "That's a good thing."

12

Duffy opened his eyes, he was laying on the hardwood floor of the bungalow, a horrible stench in the air and a painful stinging wetness on his skull. No light but the moonlight in the window and a small green light on he ceiling indicating the fire alarm was active. Duffy could not remember what happened. The last memory that rushed to his mind was of standing outside bungalow 34, his room, and contemplating three actions: flee and alert the resort authorities that someone was in his room, wait and see what would happen, or burst in and take the villain by surprise. Apparently it was the last option which he had decided upon.

Duffy rolled onto his side and pushed up until he was on hands and knees, which brought a throbbing to his temple as he rose to standing and surveyed the room. The door was open and a tempting air blew in. He stepped carefully outside and took in the fresh air, sitting on the bench there he waited for the heavy fog to lift from his mind. He checked his phone and saw it was after midnight, would the intruder return? Had they taken anything? His chips were still on his wrist, nothing missing, there was hardly anything but clothing in his room. Footsteps sounded on the boardwalk and a couple strolled by arm in arm, laughing and chatting about the fabulous play they had just seen, then the two men turned the corner and were gone. Duffy felt the back of his head, wet, his hand came back covered in blood.

Duffy abandoned the bungalow and went to the office where the night clerk assisted him in reporting the incident and gaining a new bungalow on the opposite side of the resort. He wore a knit hat to conceal the minor head wound.

"Were you struck or did you fall and hit your head?" the clerk asked.

Duffy shrugged.

"Knockout gas." the clerk said, "This type of crime is not uncommon. What is odd is that nothing was missing. But as you say, if there was nothing to take, then it makes sense nothing was taken. We will provide medical assistance. Please have a seat."

"I could not tolerate a doctor's exam at the moment."

"We are required in the event of an assault-"

"No no, I simply bumped my head. Thank you." Duffy hustled from the office, and noticing two figures clad in black strolling towards the office, took a left turn and the long way around to his new room.

Duffy carefully unlocked his new bungalow on the West side, even watching the water line for a small boat or kayak, even snorkel tube that might be sneaking up. Locking the door he left the light off and called Jameson.

"Hello!"

"Yes, hello Jameson." Duffy felt an instant burning at the cheerful greeting.

"Duffy, how are you?"

Duffy struggled to recall his anger management techniques, "Well Jameson, I'm on the trip of a lifetime."

"Oh I love Nunavut, the people are so kind and level. Seems like a good place for you to be."

"Well there's a bad apple in the bunch. I've been assaulted in my own room and my good impression of this resort is now forever tainted."

"Wretched existence! I wouldn't go to the authorities, we haven't quite got things worked out here."

"As I suspected. Do you imagine there is an extradition agreement between New Bear and Nunavut?"

"Yes, I imagine."

The conversation became silent.

"Duffy?"

"Still here. Well. I'll be moving on tonight, I have a private transport arranged. Going to the big island for some sight seeing."

"Fine, good plan. A few more days and I think we will have you back in good standing here. You know how bureaucracy works."

"Hmmm. Thank you for your hard work."

"You would do the same for me."

"I'm still having the dreams."

"How often?"

"Every night now, without fail. Every time I sleep."

"Keep a record of it."

Were the dreams the result of some drug that Jameson had given him? He showed no signs of guilt at the mention.

"Okay then, I'm off."

"May the road rise to meet you, may he wind always be at your back, and may the sun always be shining on your face."

"Miigwech. Goodbye Jameson. Keep up the good work."

As Duffy strolled back to his room he wondered if his mistrust of Jameson was based on a false intuition, which is exactly what a mind control drug would do. But then, Jameson was very intelligent, he might have access to mind control drugs. Hmmm. Duffy locked the new bungalow door and pulled the bed covers over his head. The night had been long, but there were other planets to step and stars to bounce before the sun rose again.

13

On the planet Gaeiou a full eclipse happened each night, one moon passing in front of a smaller moon and then traveling on, and for a moment the sky dimmed from two orbs to one. That night Duffy saw moons and stars in the sky of Gaeiou and other lights too, sparkles of electricity on vehicles flying towards the factory the toads and turtles occupied. Hundreds of levitating vehicles swarming towards the control tower, these were not drones, but each had a pilot, toads mostly, some piloted by turtles, all wearing black uniforms.

As the attack flew over the forest and the front security gate another swarm rose from the forest like a flock of birds united in mind. The black uniformed group of vehicles broke formation and turned away from the tower to confront the flights rising from the forest. The forest crew was random, differently shaped and colored vehicles, they swarmed past the authorities and arranged themselves hovering in the air between the control tower and the conformity forces. The two groups hovered without taking action.

"This is too much!" Xippix pulled away from the window as the broadcast feed in the control tower lit up and made attention grabbing noise, Xippix read the news: "Turtle ship captains have shut down their engines in solidarity! They drift with a standing demand that binding agreements be signed immediately or they will not deliver. They will not restart their engines until it's done!"

Pagnellopy was fixed looking out the window at the tense confrontation, but now- was that a cheer of triumph from the occupation camp by the security gate? They listened to the same news feed as the occupied tower.

"Power use has been rationed in Heart City," Xippix continued, "Everything is shut down except for emergency services."

"See the news!" Grandstar said, "Look! Toads have come out of their holes and are playing games in the streets, blocking police vehicles from coming to the plant."

Xippix stared intently at the text, "Emergency negotiations have begun between toad & turtle governments. In the South freight train engineers and workers have struck in solidarity with the ship crews. Sulfide tankers are stopped on the tracks, they have erected tents in the front and back of all trains and vow to live in them until treaties are signed."

"It's happening outside this window too." Pagnellopy watched as the air born authorities retreated back to Heart City. The forest defenders circled the tower searching for any special operatives that might have snuck thru the line.

Xippix stared bug eyed at the news feed smiling,"Huge gatherings of social justice and environmental movements, economic blocs have organized together and now set a table that we can all eat from."

Pagnellopy turned away from the window, "A new government

must arise. It must."

"What's that noise?" Xippix said, and Pagnellopy looked out the window to see a single buzzing flight, a figure approaching the tower.

"To the roof!" Grandstar said, "We don't know who it is, we may have to repel them with the fire hose!"

Grandstar, Pagnellopy, & Xippix rushed up the steel stairs to the roof and unrolled the fire hose, Pagnellopy & Xippix grabbed the hose as practiced and Grandstar stood on the spigot. Hank's ears were perked up and pointing at the flying figure, who came close enuf now to see it was a single pilot maneuvering in a small spin rotor carrying a package. Pagnellopy and Xippix lowered the hose.

"It's my First Star!" Pagnellopy said.

Pagnellopy's First Star made landing on the roof & shut off the engine, then set a package down, "I brought food and water. Do you need it?"

Grandstar clapped, "Much appreciated! We wondered what might be for supper." Grandstar & Xippix tore into the package while Hank sniffed at it.

Pagnellopy hugged their First Star and walked them aside.

"How's my Second Star?"

"I haven't seen your Second Star much, they are a big leader in the support movement. Very busy. Here, try this." Pagnellopy took a sealed food bowl, "It's been a long time since I made a Shum-Shum fly stir fry. It is passable in taste."

Pagnellopy smiled, "Thank you. I appreciate. You've had a change of heart since we last talked?"

Pagnellopy's First Star shrugged, "You Second Star and I had a talk about support. My idea of support was trying to make you act like me. I became convinced that this goal wasn't even possible."

"Logical, like a First Star should be. Tell me news! How's the outside?"

Pagnellopy's First Star shook toad head, "Resignations, bombings, backlash, streets occupied by millions, a movement is blooming. I've never lived thru anything like this. You and a very small group of people around the world have set off something that's been bottled up a long time. Now we have to deal with it, and that looks like a good thing for the future, but right now it's just a mess. Hard to tell who's winning, it's hard to tell what winning looks like. I never thot I would be an activist, but now I wake up next to your Second Star, and we start out the day thinking: what are we gonna do to make things better?"

"I love you." Pagnellopy said, "You're a good person. We're doing this together, that makes me happy. Some people lost their families when they took a stand."

"How is Xippix? Stars won't talk? I never see Ollege and Pweon anymore. They are in the opposite camp."

"They do not support Xippix's choice." Pagnellopy said.

"It is they who made the poor choice." Pagnellopy's First Star said, "People can only make decisions based on what they know, so I would say that they don't know enuf. They are intelligent people, but also very ignorant. They drive and fly on vehicles made by scientists and allow scientists to operate on their bodies, but when the same scientists tell them toads and turtles are damaging the Gaeiou they refuse to believe it."

"It's the way our minds work, skepticism is what kept our ancestors from being eaten by predators, survivors are skeptics, the people who were hard wired to be ultra trusting didn't survive to pass their genes on. So here we are, not trusting things that we cant verify with our own eyes. Nobody can force them to come out of the darkness. I know, it's a choice that I made, to become more fully aware. You have to choose this. It's not pleasant to face a truth that threatens your entire way of life."

"Wixha. My best friend. I think about it all the time. I don't know if I can ever get over what they did to us. I could be rotting in the holding ponds right now."

Pagnellopy's First Star held two toad fingers together in a sign of contemplation, "Wixha's family wasn't rich, they were paid well for infiltrating the toad & turtle group, enuf money to put Wixha thru college. Wixha couldn't resist, pressured by family. I wouldn't waste your energy holding hatred in your heart, I'm sure that

Wixha thinks about what happened every minute of the day. That kind of shame will eat a person from the inside. No, I don't envy Wixha one bit."

"We're gonna make it thru this." Pagnellopy put two arms around their First Star and held on for a good long time.

"Okay I should go now. Your Second Star wanted me to tell you that a surprise is coming."

"A good surprise?"

"If it was a bad surprise it wouldn't be a surprise because I would tell you before it happened. Your Stars have you covered."

That evening a faint glow flashed as the old airport light tower was mysteriously turned on, spinning an alternating white and green photonic beam activated by the energy workers of Heart City in solidarity with the occupation. An oddly meaningless thing to do in a world where air travel was now automated, but the old toads and turtles smiled when they saw this sign and the young ones cried out in wonder.

14

The boat ride South on New World Gulf was rough, a hurricane
had passed thru only twelve hours previous, and Duffy struggled
to keep his eyes on the horizon to prevent nausea. Choppy waters
with white capped waves provided a brutal surface for the hull to
move on, the Gulf waters flailed repeatedly like the arms and legs
of an agitated bed partner. Duffy stood on the fore deck, hands
gripping the white painted steel rail. The ferry moved at best
speed against the Southern winds, rolling left, rolling right, rising
then dropping swiftly leaving Duffy's stomach still at the previous
position two meters higher. After an hour the result was a
queasiness that Duffy was reluctant to share with the crew for fear
of appearing to be inexperienced on the water and forced to
remain below decks under sedation. The sky grew quickly dark
tho it was only mid day and rain began to fall. The rain blew
under the deck awning so Duffy moved inside where a large
number of passengers sat looking unhappy. Duffy continued on to
the cafe on the second deck and scrolled thru the food options,
selecting nachos with jalapeno cheese sauce and a full range of
extra toppings, a day for comfort food. He listened as the robo
cook came to life with a short series of audible codes, he
recognized a 315MLX model, very reliable in tough operating
conditions such as this where the floor alternated between level
and 30 degrees of tilt, but it was limited in cooking options and

presentation styles.

Duffy found a window table, the warmth of hot food and the rain outside felt good, a surge of goose bumps even struck as the zesty jalapeno spices met his digestive system. "For me, everything is gonna be okay." Duffy told himself, "The universe will not thwart happiness in my life as long as I pay close attention to avoid the numerous pitfalls."

Heading back to the lounge Duffy cheerfully held open an old style self closing bulkhead door for several people whom he exchanged pleasantries with, then about to enter the lounge he saw a vision which froze him solid: Starblaze Sturgeon sitting with a large group of thespians. Duffy immediately let go of the door and fled back to the cafe.

"How could this be?" Duffy lamented his situation as he sunk into a corner chair and pulled the knit hat down over his eyes, pretending to be sleeping, "Curse this ship for it's lack of cabin accommodations. No, forgive me ship, it's not you."

In his pocket Duffy's phone made a noise, he pulled it forth and saw the face of Starblaze smiling at him with the message, "Let's talk!"

Duffy switched off the public access setting, "All my life what have I wanted? To be left alone by all the many pestering people who imagined they knew so much about what one should do in life that they insisted on telling every other person they met all about their grand and perfect wisdom, which always seemed to emerge from a profound ignorance of the true big picture of the universe that Duffy had actually caught several glimpses at. Over many decades Duffy sought refuge from ubiquitous stupidity in the silence of abandoned buildings, public libraries, and deep ravines where the running water of a stream provided wordless murmuring of molecules to drown out the voices of human foolishness. Such places and activities provided the soil in which Duffy grew his smiles. Sometimes there was no such beautiful refuge available, only green, blue, or brown plastic single occupancy chambers for sanitary events, with their heavy scent of disinfectant and synthetic flowers. Sometimes there was only a stinking closet with crude cleaning utensils and total darkness to hide in, but for a minute or two he could huddle and breathe, often thru the mouth to avoid retching, and absorb the sounds of silence which had their residence in those small spaces. This was always Duffy's most favored society, his own. If he could squeeze into such a refuge while on the clock and making money, so much the better. This was a natural survival mechanism for a creature caught in the capitalist gears, simply occupy the bathroom until the next person came knocking and save your body a moment of gruesome toil enriching the filthy rich.

"Things are better now. A little." Duffy relaxed under cover of his voluminous knit hat with it's zig-zag stripe and let the voices of the other passengers soothe him as if they were the slow waves that caressed the beach near his home back in New Bear. A warm hand wrapped over Duffy's hand in such a way that he failed to recoil at first, and a voice spoke softly in his ear, "We really should talk. Is this a good time for you?"

Duffy sighed and surrendered to Starblaze Sturgeon, pushing out of his slouch and up with his legs his knit hat slid back into eyes open position and he stepped into his customer service armor.

"How can I help you?"

Starblaze Sturgeon took a seat next to his and leaned in, "Jameson told me about what you've received. I was shocked and suspicious because I had received something that seemed to be identical. Of course I suspected some illegal scheme involving drugs or nano mind printing, but what could anyone want with me? I am the elected leader of a radical theater troop that lives in the woods, off the grid, so we can fully immerse in our art and wild style. There seemed to be no point in manipulating me, except for pure experimentation? The population of the world has dropped drastically but there are still those kinds of people unfortunately."

Duffy's eyes bulged out as he tried to swallow all the information, "What has Jameson told you? I haven't received anything from anyone. I have nothing but a cafe and a garden and I wonder if even that remains. It is possible I have nothing at all."

"I have received the visions. When I saw you at the resort I knew I had to find out, so I searched your bungalow for evidence thinking you may have recorded the dreams. I did find something. You wrote the name on the resort stationary."

"Gaeiou." Duffy said.

Starblaze pulled the paper from her pocket, "The planet Gaeiou. I have received this vision too."

Duffy shifted in his seat, noting the two exits from the room and four other people seated nearby. Shared vision or not: this was the villain who assaulted him in his room!

15

"Let's back up." Duffy shifted in his corner seat, forward on the chair so more of his weight was on his toes, ready to leap and defend himself, "Why did you make that play about me?"

"It was Davidoon's turn to propose a performance and he loves high concept. Overheard my conversation with Jameson and wrote the play overnight, insisted we perform it when you arrived at the colony." Starblaze sighed, "It may be true that artists should not live in colonies like ants, you get a dozen people tugging on something and it doesn't matter if it's a good idea or not, it's going to move."

"And the assault in my bungalow?" Duffy held her gaze and prepared for an outburst."

"I never touched you."

"I woke up with a bloody wound on my head."

"I didn't realize. You burst into the room so wildly screaming that I was frightened terribly which cued my protection unit, automatic knockout gas dispersal, which I have systemic immunity to. When I turned around you were flat on the floor."

"And you left me there."

"No, I checked your vitals, the protection unit does that automatically, not legal to have one that doesn't do that. I knew you were okay. Duffy, I'm not a barbarian. Please forgive the trespass, I had to know if you were real or some nefarious force. These dreams have taken over my life. Now Duffy, I have questions for you. Why did you follow me to the resort?"

"What!" Duffy flinched, "I was fleeing from you and your troupe, and it seems a vicious belch of fate brought me on a duplicate course!"

"And here we are. Wondering if toads and turtles are real."

Duffy recoiled, was this maniac the only person on Earth who shared his strange dream torment? Was Starblaze real? Jameson suggested an emergent mental illness. From inside a mentally ill mind, was it possible to reference reality as a singular truth? Was that ever possible?

"Life has not taught me to be a trusting person." Duffy said.

Starblaze Sturgeon leaned back in her chair and laughed loud, heads turned and then heads swung back to their original positions as tho spring loaded, "And you think I live in the woods because I have faith in a city full of thieves, murderers, and patriarchs? Put yourself inside my shirt for a moment. Here you are, some character from New Bear on the run from the law and who seems to be stalking me."

Duffy sat back in his chair and held up one hand, "Say no more. I am enlightened. Please sit with me and have tea. Tell me when your visions began."

16

The Gulf ferry arrived at destination and bumped gently into the dock as the crew threw shore lines and deployed a ramp to immediately transfer passengers to the waiting Southbound train. Despite the epiphany Duffy had at the end of his convo on the ferry with Starblaze Sturgeon, he still dead-locked the door to his berth on the sleeper train as there were a dozen radical thespians roaming the halls. Climbing into bed that evening knowing he was not alone in the world with his vision Duffy felt a strong glow expanding from his center, an experience which one doesn't miss until that day you feel it and the empty space inside is filled which you thot had already been full but was actually full of emptiness and nothing.

The train rolled South on gentle suspension and seamless trackage, the slight sensation of movement rocked Duffy to sleep. Somewhere inside the harmonic sounds of the train gently spinning along a song was playing, three notes in the low range of a piano thrummed out the skipping jig of a bass line, the sound you might hear in your mind when stepping outside too meet the morning of a sunny day, a melody full of arm in arm joy and smiles. The song bloomed with the addition of a high melody, wooden keys triggering soft felt hammers on hard steel strings, keyed out notes that painted a picture of a bird in triumphant flight, of toads dancing with shoulders and hips, and turtles moving along at full speed towards a hopeful future. On this Long Summer day all three suns were shining on Gaeiou.

Pagnellopy walked with Xippix & Hank in a wild wood, birds of many kinds called out to them from tree branches, wild cats lay sunning themselves in clearings and the tops of bluffs, a creek flowing nearby splashed with spawning fish. Soon they arrived at a small lake and immediately went swimming. Pagnellopy swam out to a big rock and set up fly fishing with a small folding rod, Xippix walked down the shore a bit and began turtle dive fishing. Hank sat behind Pagnellopy, guarding the perimeter and listening to the chittering of a chipmunk somewhere safely high up in a Forevergreen Tree. Xippix soon returned from fishing, chewing on something.

"Feels good to be in the country." Pagnellopy said.

"Long way from the Holding Ponds."

"Long way."

"And may we always stay a safe distance from them!"

"This is exactly what I thot about every day to get me thru it."

Someone was walking down the rocky trail and into the meadow next to the lake, moving out of the tall grass they saw it was Wixha.

"I came here looking for you." Wixha said.

Pagnellopy jigged the rod, "What have you to say?"

"I came to apologize." Wixha turned their turtle hands out, "I let my parents push me into a decision that I now regret, I was afraid, and then I was greedy. They played me, I could only think of my own selfish desires, and in the end I found out I lost the only things I actually cared about. So, Pagnellopy, and Xippix, I'm sorry. I hope someday you'll be my friend again. Or at least, just not hate me."

"I have no intention of hating you, Wixha. It is the hater who falls ill. I will put my passion elsewhere. How did you find us?"

"Your Second Star drove me here."

Pagnellopy looked up at the sky, "Good night! An age of wonders. I accept your apology Wixha, for myself. For the rest of the movement, you'll have to address them directly."

"Mmm." Xippix's turtle eyes narrowed, "Let me sleep on it."

"It may take me some time to trust you again." Pagnellopy said, "I think I could. Maybe."

Wixha gave Pagnellopy a turtle smile: "That's the best I could hope for. Okay. See you in school!" Wixha turned and skipped quickly up the trail.

"Waters!" Xippix held up a ceramic drinking flask, Pagnellopy raised their own flask and they drank simultaneously, then exchanged flasks and drank, then handed back the flasks and drank again, completing the Toast of Three Suns, a celebratory tradition of Gaeiou.

"What next, will Chartles come along and offer us a home

cooked meal?" Pagnellopy jigged their rod and laughed.

"I think some of the goodness left in life may take a little longer to simmer out."

"Lets stroll around the lake." Pagnellopy said.

"A circumnavigational victory lap."

While walking they came upon a wild cat sunning itself on a large smooth boulder, it's fur was solid black and it slow blinked at them. Hank the dog approached the cat, "Hello cat. Have you seen any Chipmunks in the wood today? They make the most interesting music."

The cats head glowed with a golden aura, "Hmmmm. Yes. Fascinating." The cat excused itself from the convo to join a circle of wild cats in a larger meadow by the lake. The cats arranged themselves in proximity to each other and a golden glow suffused the air around them. Pagnellopy, Xippix, and Hank stopped to watch, from the path they could see space and time become fluid and slowly spin above the wild cats.

"We have to share our story the way the wild cats do, together, and send it out to all of Gaeiou. We have to get our story out or else it might be forgotten in the chaos and the whole struggle would be for nothing. We must not fail to inspire."

"If we do that, it will go farther then Gaeiou, it will go everywhere, in everything. That is sacred. I don't think they will help us."

"We have to transgress the sacred and share our knowledge. Everything is going to change. We can stop a lot of suffering by doing this. The wheels are turning and we can make sure the revolutions continue. We may offend some people. We may be in danger. There is always a price to pay to end suffering because some people are deeply invested in the continuation of suffering for their personal benefit."

"You speak what is true."

17

Duffy opened his eyes feeling refreshed in the moving sleeper train as it rolled slowly side to side, headed toward home in the city of New Bear on the Western shore of New World Gulf. He rose up and pulled the heavy curtain back, outside a thick window the sky poured rain. Duffy had reserved a room on the East side of the train facing the open water for when they emerged from hills and forest he would be able to see the ever changing water of the ocean, sometimes bright green under stormy skies, sometimes a dark blue under slanting sun rays, a blue so deep almost violet, endless shades in this spectrum, and then sometimes capped with angry white under wild winds. Today it was rolling white topped waves crashing in great cataclysms against the ancient basaltic rock of the magmatic upwelling that was the continent. Water falling from the sky and rolling in the gulf, the same water that ten thousand years ago moved in a frozen sheet across the land, slow working the old rock as it went like a most careful and grand artisan. What artistic vision did today's storm strive towards, Duffy considered the rows of endless waves moving towards shore to make their wild splash grinding sand on stone and fly white foaming passion into the air raining down on black rock which seemed unaffected by the action, but somewhere down there under the liquid a tiny grain broke loose from the continental shield like a tear from the eye of a creator.

A knock rang on his cabin door and Duffy realized he was naked, "A moment please!"

Duffy dressed and opened the door to find the train steward patiently waiting, the medicine pouch strings that went around his neck and disappeared down his shirt were similar to styles of tribes in Duffy's old home state of Minnesota, "Hurricane on the way. I see you've got a window weather report so you might have guessed already. Hurricane has deviated from the usual track following the Pacific current up the West side of Greenland and cut across the mainland direct into the Gulf, slightly weakened but still going good. Could get a bump from the warm waters and be upgraded by the time it makes landfall again in a few hours. Storm surge could flood the tracks and wind could knock the train over so we'll have to go into the hole and wait it out."

"Ah. Bonus vacation time. Miigwech."

"Miigwech."

The steward smiled the broad smile in the tradition of laughing-disease-giver-in-the-face and continued down the hall knocking on other cabin doors.

Duffy closed his door and adjusted his hasty fashion, then packed up with anticipation of a wild ride and possible evacuation to high ground. Checking his phone he found no signal available, the storm had stirred up such a thick blanket of ionized particles that nothing could get thru. Truly it would be unfortunate if any accident occurred, there would be no possibility of calling for rescue. Presumably the railroad had a central headquarters where such things as train movements and hurricanes were co-ordinated, but one should never fully trust a bureaucratic system, only the individuals in it, which was often a great unknown. Who was the engineer of the train, responsible for all their lives? Unknown. The modern age had many uncertainties, each new morning often brought drastic changes in what previously had been considered somewhat permanent.

Duffy packed a slim bag, water, food, a shock defensive tool, a hat light, a micro thin all weather jacket, and an automatic inflatable life preserver. One did not survive without being prepared, and one's ancestors would not smile upon a sudden clumsy death.

A vital element of survival was having functional circles of friends and allies, so Duffy left his cabin and strolled to the dining car to meet with Starblaze Sturgeon for breakfast. She was already there with a crew of bug eyed thespians far too awake at this time of day for Duffy's liking.

"What's in the bag?" she asked.

"Dietary cookies. You never know what fare might be offered on these trains. If they leave town without some essential ingredients, there's no going back. The entrees are sometimes inedible."

The breakfast was a delicious quiche of onion, garlic, spinach, goosefoot leaves, topped with fresh ground pepper served with a side salad of spring greens in a subtle vinaigrette. Usually Duffy would never eat greens for breakfast but with the quiche it went well. After a cup of earl gray tea Duffy began to enjoy the lively convo between members of the troupe, almost forgetting the approaching storm.

The train ambled slowly thru foothills and into forested valleys, rain continued and the sun was hidden. The train slowed and crawled into a steep vale and then rolled to a gentle stop. Duffy looked out the window, appreciating the view which might be theirs for awhile.

"Looks like a good spot to sit it out." Starblaze said, "Beautiful here. We might go for a walk outside before the storm hits."

A young man from the troupe responded, "If we wait until the wall of the hurricane passes we can go for a walk in the eye of the hurricane! It wont be raining then, we'll stay dry."

"There will be a Festival of Silence you can bet!" another actor said with wide eyes.

"Let's do it all!" Starblaze slapped her hands on the old wooden table and laughed.

Outside they walked on rough rock ballast which crunched underfoot as they moved up the tracks toward the head end of the passenger train. The plan was to get a look at the engines and catch some gossip from the unit crew.

"What did your parents do?" Starblaze asked Duffy.

"My folks built greenhouses in old Montana and moved to the domes in Minnesota after the Montana project was done." Duffy said, "My mom was an architect and my father a fabricator, they were like a manifestation of their generation, totally different minds working towards this one goal. Passionately! Failure was not an option. They had two children who needed a functional world to live, so they tried to build it."

"Where does your sister live?"

"She lived in Iowa when she was killed in a lightening storm."

"Oh."

"Statistics. It has to happen to someone."

A monarch butterfly moved across the air in front of them and made landing on a shrub near the woods.

"There's a miracle." Duffy said, "Scientists figured out how to move the Monarchs winter home to Colorado, and they bought it! Now they migrate from there all the way to Greenland to mate."

"It does warm the heart to see a success when you know the extinction list is higher than you can count."

"Even if the polar bears could have survived it would have been difficult living side by side with them."

"I hear the white bears have been seen West of here, adapting to being on solid land year round."

Duffy swallowed, "I don't think I need to ask what they are eating."

Ahead the row of passenger cars disappeared into the dark round mouth of a tunnel in a pine tree covered mountain, the shape of the dark cavern slightly illuminated by a glow emanating from train car windows which stretched deep into the tunnel.

"The whole front end is safely tucked away." Duffy said.

"It seems that our economy tickets do not afford us the luxury of being out of the hurricane." Starblaze stopped and surveyed the scene. A small waterfall to the right of the tunnel entrance made for a charming tableau.

"A resort could be built right here, quite beautiful. Save us the trouble of taking the ferry all the way to Nunavut." Duffy smiled as he looked up at the towering white pines. A noise rose from the woods, a howl, long and clear, ending with staccato yips.

"Coyowolves." Starblaze whispered, "They've smelled the cafe car exhaust. If there are no scraps to be had they will settle for a slow moving elder or a drunk."

"Hmm. Not it!" Duffy scanned the tree line, imagining every fallen tree or root ball to be a creature.

"Once we were the top of the food chain. We've slipped a bit. Numbers aren't in our favor anymore. Living out in the woods like I do, it's humbling."

"Not too many visitors for the coyowolves along this stretch of tracks. Back to the car then?" Duffy turned to look behind them.

"They wouldn't be howling if they were hunting us, but we may as well be safe, there could be more than one pack."

As they turned away from the mountain the sky was darker than when they had left the train. Starblaze spoke, "Have you seen me in your dreams?"

Duffy recalled a dream memory as tho it were a waking memory and he inhaled quickly. Starblaze had been in his dreams but he immediately wondered if the memory had just been manufactured the instant she asked the question.

"I believe the answer is yes. It should be no shock considering the importance you have in my present life."

Starblaze nodded while walking, "But it's more than that. You also have been a player on the stage in my little singular skull of a theater. I see you when I sleep, you are there with me watching the lives of the people on planet Gaeiou."

Duffy felt dizzy, "I know we have already established this, but it still disturbs me. I live a solitary life most of the time, I have my regulars at the cafe and some few friends, that's all. I read, I listen. I share my thots sometimes but always at my choosing. This mutual connection is difficult to trust. I imagine you are successfully plying some advanced puzzelry on my mind and I have been taken in by the trick. You are skilled in convincing people, a story teller, I am correct? It is your trade."

Starblaze Sturgeon laughed, "With cynics in the audience my job is difficult. Please, there exists technology that could fool us enuf to make us feel the tingle of real magic, but why? What would be the point of throwing us together with this story of toads and turtles, what use? No one is making a profit on this. No one could be gaining power. It's like a prank, but where's the humor?"

"The good thing about our shared experience is that it seems to lessen the possibility of this being an emergent mental illness."

"Self awareness lessens the chance of several mental illnesses but not all. We are on the cutting edge, let's find a third opinion before we present our paper."

The rear end of the passenger train sat on a short bridge that spanned a plummeting gorge, far below was a raging rapid, the misty bottom of a wild waterfall. Halfway across this old steel bridge stood a hooded figure holding something substantial against the thick black railing, the figure was agitated and punched the thing against the railing while cursing loudly.

The agitated figure concluded their violence with the object and flipped it over the railing and into the abyss it tumbled, as it tumbled down an arm and leg protruded, or was it only clothing falling out of an open bag? An immediate answer was lost in the branches below that obscured the bottom of what would be certain death.

A scream accompanied the last moments of the falling bag while the figure on the bridge held their hands up to the sky. It as not obvious to Duffy or Starblaze exactly where the scream emanated from: the hooded figure still on the bridge, or the thing that now churned against ancient black rocks in the roiling waters below.

18

The figure was cloaked and they couldn't see a face until Duffy uttered a noise of shock. The figure turned towards them, exposing his pale white face which burned into their eyes before he fled, dashing up the steps of he nearest passenger car. Starblaze and Duffy ran to the scene and looked over the railing into the impossible mist below where nothing could be seen. They entered the rail car where the figure had gone but there was no one in the hall.

"I will search forward, you search back." Starblaze said.

"Agreed, but take no action. We should not incite this fellow to further violence."

Duffy walked calmly down the hall, past doors and windows of sleeping berths, peeking into any that was open, receiving numerous frowns and downward eyebrows as he went, saying repeatedly, "Sorry! Wrong room."

There were very few white people on the train, it seemed a reasonable proposition to find this person. Soon Duffy was in the dining car scanning the faces having lunch in the oddly unmoving train car, a last meal before the storm. Duffy moved to the middle of the car, looking at every face, and approached a four top which was occupied by only one person.

"Hello." Duffy said to the hooded figure staring stiffly at a menu, the man turned his face up and Duffy's original suspicion that this character, and his activities by the bridge, had been the latest plot by Starblaze and the theater group to torment him was eliminated. Duffy recognized the skinny white man under the cloak.

"Crowded in here isn't it." the man recovered and smiled, "Everyone wondering if this might be their last supper."

Duffy swallowed and pulled up one of the chairs, "Yes, let's have something. Hungry?" Duffy picked up a menu and keyed his account.

"I am hungry." the blond man said, "Do you suggest anything?"

"I'll order two Indian Taco Platters, a classic of the Native American diaspora, Northern Soul Food. Tasty fry bread forms the outside of the Indian taco, and is actually a creative use of wheat flour rations the government made Indians eat while they were unable to hunt traditional game while being incarcerated in concentration camps by the European invaders."

"Your treat? I won't be rude and refuse then. Thank you, I'm honored." the man leaned closer to Duffy, "It makes no difference I know, but I am first generation immigrant to this continent. Born in Wales. The village doesn't exist anymore, it's now under the Pacific Ocean. Might as well be Atlantis."

"The situation is much changed now." Duffy sighed and leaned back, "A week ago I witnessed a ship of refugees sunk to the bottom of New World Gulf. I wonder if the oppressed have become the oppressors, I don't much like some of this New World we have reclaimed, or inherited, or seized, but we are dealing with a global situation largely created by the white man. The planet is a chaotic mess, rapidly changing. Someday the privileges may shift again."

A door o the diner car opened and closed, a louder sound than usual since the train was at rest. Starblaze strode to the table and sat next to Duffy.

"Room for one more even," the refugee said to Starblaze, "I do love making new friends in the dining car."

"Hungry?" Duffy handed her the menu, "Let me introduce you to the fellow who came to my cafe and was chased out by tribal police. Perhaps we should formally introduce ourselves since it seems our paths will cross again, probably in court."

The robo server approached their table in that moment and with a short song announced the arrival of food and deposited place settings.

"I find talking while eating to be entirely gruesome," the man said, "I hope we can enjoy this warm meal first."

Duffy and Starblaze watched carefully as the man picked up a taco from his plate and began eating. No blood on his hands, no signs of distress. When his mouth was empty the man thanked Duffy, "Delicious. I could happily grow fat eating these."

"How did you escape from the authorities in New Bear?"

The man smiled, "As you said, the situation is much changed now. I think it would be best for us to decline a tedious visit to the museum of the recent past and simply remain in the present moment. Here we are, stranded on a train awaiting a storm, trapped with good food and good company, let's not focus on unpleasant things."

"One thing," Starblaze leaned in, "What were you doing out on that bridge a moment ago?"

The man smiled again, "A moment ago? Another age in another world. I'm a private man, shall we speak of something filthy and rude next? Let's forget about it, there's no harm done."

Starblaze slapped the menu and gripped the table as tho she might fling it into the air and start throwing punches.

"I see that you are agitated. Let me put your mind to rest with one single word which will reveal to you that we are on the same side, or at least that we share a vision-"

The man's mouth snapped shut as a flood of people burst thru a door at the end of the passenger car, the group followed two muscular crew members brandishing non-lethal weapons. One of the passengers sprang from behind and pointed at the blond man sitting with Duffy and Starblaze, "There he is! That's the murderer!" The blond man jumped up and the table tipped, food and drinks spilled onto Starblaze and Duffy's laps, causing them to jump to their feet in shock which put them directly in the line of fire. Hidden behind his dining companions, the blond man pulled the red emergency exit handle on the window which flopped outward, wild winds from the increasing hurricane blew hard into the car. The fugitive jumped out the window and was reborn into the world just as the crew opened up with their stun weapons and being slightly inexperienced put half the dining car into an unconscious state which was instantly irritating to the server bots who switched to emergency mode. Food and drink orders were abandoned to comfort the screaming and sobbing passengers and to assist in removing food from the mouths of unconscious people who were choking in their undignified positions slumped over tables and sprawled across the floor.

19

Duffy entered a dream loaded with zesty spices, a market with stalls and carts that displayed large open bins full of brightly colored powders, a disordered rainbow assortment which caused his eyes to bulge and nose to tingle. There were others in the dream with him, Starblaze! Yes it couldn't be anyone else. Others surrounding, a dozen unidentified spirits from Earth floating the same direction as he, blown by an unseen wind. But Starblaze was close to him, he could feel her there, bonded. They flew above the market and into the bulk dried insects quarter where massive baskets full of perfectly dried Shum-Shum flies hung from round hollow-wood racks. Laid on tables underneath were the smoked and water weed wrapped Hagel Tongue Worms stacked neatly in tall pyramids. Floating on they passed over large barrels full of live stock, mini Tokokeels and tasty Margine Smelts swimming in lazy circles.

Toad Pagnellopy was carefully netting the small fish and plopping them into traveling water sacks while turtle Xippix watched, "The cats should enjoy our gift." Pagnellopy said, "I wonder if they will allow us to participate in the circle."

"Your Grandstar heard rumors of it happening when he was young. Nothing but rumors. Hardly a precedent."

"The cats must think it's important. They must." Pagnellopy held open a pack for Xippix, "They have a collective wisdom that spans multiple species. If their consensus is against us, we must completely rethink our strategies."

"Always good to stop and look at the big picture."

Xippix now held open a pack for Pagnellopy to tuck in a water sack loaded with fish, "Have you traveled far with these water sacks before? Will they leak?"

"Yes I've been hiking with these before." Xippix paid the vendor and carefully lifted a double sided shelf pack onto turtle back, "We got this!" Xippix smiled and with packs on they strolled purposefully from the market.

The road to Light Hollow was very narrow and mostly single file thru long forests and up and down several small mountains. The entire Forest of Light was protected by law, no roads or development was allowed, only foot, paw, hoof, and wing travel was allowed. Pagnellopy's toad feet hopped easy over boulders and large roots. Xippix's clawed turtle feet made small scraping noises as they scrabbled over the rough parts of the trail. In the dim understory of the forest they saw a sixty knobbed Rochie cross the trail and pause majestically on it's two muscular legs, looking at the visitors from the lowlands before strutting on and disappearing down a trial bordered by thick brush, a path that Pagnellopy and Xippix would never have noticed if the buck hadn't allowed them to see it.

Pagnellopy and Xippix paused at a scenic overlook for a small lunch. The sun shone down thru Crystal Candy Bush Trees and warmed the old smooth rock exposed on the mountain top where the two relaxed their limbs and bodies.

"The first hour I was suffering but now it feels good." Xippix stretched limbs to full length from turtle shell then rolled back to sitting position, "Exercise makes you high. I forget about that. All that sitting in circles and polite conversation. Intellectually stimulating and socially essential. Also physiologically stultifying and ultimately not stimulating to the brain as the brain is connected to the body."

"The philosopher Jaques liked to play Leap Toad while having conversation specifically to promote intense sharpness of the mind." Pagnellopy said.

"Leap Toad! I never tried. A turtle doing leap toad looks undignified, it would be a distraction not and enhancement."

"Whatever." Pagnellopy choked on a dried Shum-Shum fly.

"You think we could have just a couple freshies?" Xippix eyed the pack with the Margin Smelt safely packed in their water bags.

Pagnellopy shook their head, "We need every one. If it looks like we are being less than generous it might not go well."

A shadow passed over their picnic spot and they looked up, a massive Green Bosque soared over and banked left, circling the mountain top.

"Wow." Pagnellopy whispered, "I've never seen a Green Bosque so close."

"If I was alone I might be scared right now. That is huge!"

"They never attack two or more. It's unheard of." Pagnellopy's four eyes scanned the entire sky.

"So don't wander off now, ya hear?" Xippix laughed.

The two packed their bags and continued down the overgrown and rocky trail, frequently looking to the sky and searching the forest horizon for what wildness they might see next.

20

Duffy opened his eyes to a face of deep lines and crow feet, black and gray hair braided and pulled back into a bun that rose straight up from her head like Bear Lodge mountain in Wyoming.

"Welcome back." the face said to him, "Water?" she held a cup out.

Duffy rose up on his elbows, unfolding as tho emerging from hibernation, muscles stiff and a strange taste in his mouth like that smell right before it pours rain. Duffy sat up in a room that was not his, alone with the woman who was a stranger, the door to the sleeping berth closed, the train still unmoving. Duffy took the water and drank, he could feel it flowing down such a dry throat that it was like he had never drank water before. The strange smell faded.

"Okay, how do you know him?"

"What?" Duffy squinted at the lights on their maximum settings.

"And why did he run."

Duffy felt acute awareness that he was sitting on comfortable cotton sheets that were not his own.

"Oh." Duffy bulged his eyes and surveyed the room again, "You're the inspector?"

"Yes." she frowned, "Now I have answered a question so it is your time to reciprocate. But first, let's do a health check. How are you feeling? Are you okay?"

"I'm alright. A little disoriented."

"Good. Now tell me how you know this man that has so hastily abandoned my train."

Duffy felt a flood of nausea and a slight pulsating began in his left temple, "The man at our table? Don't know. You know how it is, dining on a train car, limited space, everyone shares tables."

"Yes. The staff tells me you had a conversation while sitting with this man."

"As one does in a crowded dining car on a train."

"I am told the dining car was at half capacity when you were seated. Robotic server logs correlate this staff observation. You knew the man well enuf to sit and converse with him. Let me say, you are not being charged with anything at the moment but if you assist a murderer in escaping from legal prosecution you will be charged along with him and that charge is the same as the murder charge. So please tell me where you know him from."

"Murder. The man is a suspect?"

"Yes, we have witnesses. Half an hour ago. Murder. It's illegal." she leaned in, "Help me out Duffy! What have you got?"

Duffy reached for the water glass and drained it, "Excuse me, I've never been stunned before, there is some dis-orientation involved. Shouldn't I receive proper counsel before being questioned?"

"As you wish." the inspector rose from her seat, "You may remain in his locked berth on house arrest until we reach New Bear."

"Wait! I understand, I only wish my request for counsel to be on record. I will tell you what I know. We saw the same thing the other passengers saw, but we were not sure what we saw. Perhaps a case of theft or fraud or even just littering. The man seems to be struggling with a mental illness."

"Who is we?" the inspector held her open hands in the air.

"Starblaze and I, we saw the blond man throw something over the bridge, then he ran inside the train and we followed him."

"Starblaze Sturgeon! I knew it. I love her work. The fourth wall doesn't exist in her mind, her theater doesn't even have walls, or a roof! Sometimes I'll be investigating something and I think, am I in one of Starblaze Sturgeon's plays? And I look around like, where's the cameras! It's distracting."

"Yes, she is very distracting." Duffy felt sweat forming on his head and shifted uncomfortably on the bed.

"Okay we've established that I am a fan of Starblaze Sturgeon. So then you sat down with the killer for some lunch."

"No, we didn't see him kill anyone, we weren't sure what we had seen, but it seemed suspicious so we followed him."

"You decided to conduct your own investigation."

"Oh dear. Maybe I should wait for counsel to advise me."

"All within your rights of course, but no worries Duffy, we performed some simple scans while you were out and can release you to house custody on the train." the inspector pulled out a tablet with charts displayed on it, "Amygdala scan shows no shrinkage and is within range of normal activity, left right activity within range, glandular motion normal range, you are not at risk of violence and all the Neuro-legal requirements have been satisfied. I just need you to remain on the train for further questioning and to help find the killer. The passenger manifest shows that all are accounted for, no missing persons declared here or in any population center back up the line. That doesn't mean there hasn't been a murder, just that there's no record of it. There's no blood on the bridge and no body in the gorge. It's lucky for all of us that the train was stopped when this happened, usually these murders happen at full speed and we would have to go back scanning kilometers of woods along the tracks for the body."

"Oh! How often does this happen? The brochure said nothing about frequent murders on the train!"

"It's best not to publicize such things, people get bad ideas. So we can hold you for 24 hours but after that we must legally let you go." the inspector rose to her feet, "I appreciate your help. I'm done with the bad cop routine now, my intuition and the data says you weren't involved in a crime, so just try and relax. Stay on the train until New Bear and don't switch your berth. Okay?"

"Well, I'm feeling some anxiety now. I imagine my next appearance in the dining car will cause a stir."

The inspector waved her hand, "I will make a small announcement. It may help those who still have any trust in authority."

Wind rocked the train car side to side as she moved for the door, howling against the round metal and playing symphonics thru the small cracks of outside doors and windows.

"Stay on the train." she pointed a finger, "And if you see the blond man, inform me immediately, contact any of the crew or a server-bot."

Duffy lifted a hand to say goodbye and let it drop, turning his head to look out the window at the rocks and tree roots of the mountain pass, "There seems to be little reason to venture out. Perhaps I will order in."

The inspector smiled with her hand on the door latch, "Well, there's no where for you to go out here. If you want to celebrate the eye of the hurricane with the rest, go on out."

"I've been there, done that, I'm over it."

Duffy stepped out to met Starblaze in the aft lounge. Passengers and crew in the halls followed his movement from the corner of their eyes and leaned into their conversation, it was clear they were discussing how the accomplice of a killer walked free among them. Once a whisper of "Murder!" touched his ears followed by a blast of wind from the approaching hurricane that shook and rattled the train and someone behind him stifled a scream, as if the killer now had ultimate power and controlled the weather. Duffy rolled his eyes. Strolling into the dining car he noticed an unpleasant acrid odor: vomit, feces, and cleaning solutions. The muscles in his neck tightened as he remembered the blast from the stun gun.

Starblaze sat in a comfortable lounge sofa facing out the rear windows of the last car on the train, outside the tree lined tracks stretched into the distance and vanished at a point, the sky above dark and moving.

Duffy sat beside her, "Were you scanned?"

"Yes. I had a lovely time with Miss Inspector. So fascinating to see images of my own brain. There is still mystery in the world, as long as we have the mind. Did you look at your scans?"

"No, I didn't think to seek any pleasure in my encounter with the authorities."

Duffy and Starblaze ordered a good dinner as the sun set too rapidly, sending warm rays for a moment under the vast swirling cloud layers. Thru large windows they watched the pine forest outside the dining car dancing under storm winds, wildly bent in a single direction as the hurricane rolled in. Sheets of rain undulated in waves and washed over the train windows.

"The eye is small." Starblaze said while watching the news on the wall, "Wont be much time for the Festival of Silence."

"Good." Duffy looked up at the screen, "I've been thru two eyes in New Bear and it's about as irritating as a New Years party."

"At least the second eye wall shows up soon to wash the drunks away!"

"It's our version of the running of the bulls. Head butting a hurricane. Incredible to see someone go from being completely rational to fully hallucinating in less than a minute. I am not impressed."

"Duffy, you're such a tick. The Festival of Silence is not traditional but it does seem to have some cathartic effect for the people who participate in it."

A small group was gathering at the bar in the aft lounge, mixing drinks and pouring them into tall transparent tubes with valves on the bottom.

"Those are from an old robo cook!" Duffy said, "I hope they haven't dismantled our food supply for this hideous festival."

"I've had enuf of your negativity Duffy. Please retain further critique of the festival until it is over. My ears will be closed until then."

Everyone in the gathering was attired in tight fitting and brightly colored outfits made of a single piece of extruded synthetic fabric, the type of outfit you could keep in a miniature capsule in your bag or pocket until needed. One festival participant pointed outside and all turned to witness a large tree crash down as the eye wall ripped thru the forest, bending all the trees into elbows. The crowd in the lounge hooted and danced as the storm front thrashed. In fifteen minutes the winds slacked and ended, the group quieted to whispers and slowly tip toed down the steps and out of the train to an open rocky flat area between the train and the forest.

Duffy and Starblaze followed. In the distance the dark clouds moved, a white noise, while next to the train water dumped by the winds dripped loudly from trees. The sun had set as the eye wall passed over them, directly above them the brightest stars and planets could be seen.

The group of celebrants danced quietly as the eye moved overhead, then lifted their tubes to the sky and sucked liquid contents down. They doubled over and cursed, some beat each other with the tubes, some reared back and cried out to the sky. One began a single sustained vocal note, and was joined by all the others in a haunting chorus which resonated thru the train. What followed was complete chaos. Dancing indistinguishable from wrestling, running and jumping, singing that could also be called screaming. Many of them now were no longer colorful but were the same shade of brown after rolling in the fresh mountain mud. All of them stumbled and became rubber legged crawling back to the cache of tubes where they ingested more of the liquid and went leaping again into the air. A breeze came up, this time blowing from the opposite direction. A person wearing a rainbow colored tight suit and who had only been observing the ritual blew a very loud air horn and held their arms up in a V shape. Duffy returned to the train to find a good window spot in the lounge car before the muddied celebrants returned.

The robo servers had just finished placing absorbent towels on all the furniture when Starblaze Sturgeon came limping into the lounge using an empty tube as a crutch and sunk into a recliner next to Duffy. Mud was streaked thru her hair and muddy hand prints made up her face, she closed her eyes and breathed deeply in and out, "That was a good one."

"Really." Duffy pursed his lips.

"Embrace the chaos Duffy."

Outside the windows of the car the wind began bending the tops of trees, now in the opposite direction as before, seeming to bring the balance back in the spines of the poor evergreens.

After some time of howling wind Duffy decided the sound of his voice would be comforting, "We're more than halfway thru this wall now I think!"

A crashing noise came from the side of the train that was against the mountain, pressed against the windows they saw the branches of evergreen trees, their needles screeching back and forth on the glass.

Starblaze's smile went away and her eyes opened when a heavy thump shook the train, "Waa! That's bad."

The train jolted even harder when a tree landed on the lounge car leaving a trunk shaped depression on the metal ceiling above the window. Passengers sitting there flinched downward and looking up they quickly stood and moved away.

"I may have been selfish hoarding this window seat." Duffy said.

Screams could be heard from the next car up and the train continued to rumble as if being repeatedly struck. Duffy was up, "The doorways are stronger, to the door!" he dashed to the end of the car and ducked into an alcove next to the exit. Looking back he saw the muddy jumpsuit wearing and exhausted from drugs Starblaze crawling on the carpet and he ran back to help her to safety. Strange how one channels their parents in time of crisis, Duffy's mother being an architect and his father a fabricator, without them he would not have known that this was the strongest part of the train car. In the terrifying noise of the storm his parents manifested and whispered in his ears and kissed his forehead.

Other passengers joined them in the space and huddled together, Starblaze Sturgeon was exhausted from the ritual and clung to Duffy's coat like a baby, "It may be hard for you to believe but I have never been in the eye before, I had to dance!" she laughed wildly, "I thot, oh, maybe I'll just drink half a tube but

116

then the storm master hands you a tube and what are you gonna do, sip on it? No, you drink the whole damn thing."

The ground shook, the train rattled, rocks and trees landing on the roof sounded like bombs and guns. A window broke and rain, rocks, and tree branches blew hard into the lounge where people huddled under tables and overturned love seats.

Starblaze began crying, "I've left too many things undone."

Duffy felt rage at this woe the blond refugee had brought to his life, the very reason he was on this death train, but then hot tears arrived as tho his body were trying to conceal itself inside the swirling raindrops of the angry storm. The train car lifted and moved as tho the very tracks had become molten.

Duffy wondered, "Where will tonight's dreaming take me if I do not survive this?"

After forever the landslide ceased. They listened to the crying and the rain and the wind. Soon it was only the crying and even that stopped.

21

Duffy walked on air. He was surrounded by friends who were also walking in the sun light filled sky, treading on invisible staircases. Duffy walked on invisible stairs that no one had taught him existed, somehow he just knew they were there, invisible stairs criss-crossing the sky. Not so joyfully liberating as actual wind in your hair dream flying, but very few people could walk on air so it was a moment of exhilaration. However, it seemed like no one on the ground ever looked up so the victory was lonesome. Easy to get lost on invisible stairs branching off in all directions, soon you're upside down headed the wrong way.

Duffy looked around, where was this? It felt like he had been climbing for hours. Below was a jumbo forest of sprawled leaves that from high up looked like a comfy bed after being ruffled up by your favorite dog, or somewhere under that green blanket a cat was hiding, careful not to lay on them, or move your feet too fast.

The invisible stairways seemed impossible to fall off, a very good thing.

Here was a sunny clearing in the dense forest and Duffy found himself climbing down, seeing some animals curled up and stretched out in the sun sleeping there, it seemed like they were very close but it took a long time to walk down the stairs and Duffy realized that actually the cats were very large and that's why he could see them from so far away. The closer he got to the ground the larger the animals loomed until he was there standing in the grass with the big cats sunning themselves. Duffy saw they were as tall as a basketball player on Earth, but much fatter and furrier.

"Merow?" one of the cats stretched and sat up, looking at Duffy, then another head rose up out of the tall grass and it's aura began to show, a bright light surrounding it's head and then around the first cat too. The big cats sauntered toward Duffy and he became afraid and fled into the sky, further than he thot they could jump. The cats stopped and stared up at him with their bright golden auras sending out illuminating rays which awoke the other cats in the clearing. The original cat to notice Duffy raised a paw in the sky, Duffy wondered, was it saying hello? Then the cat put a back foot in the air and began walking up the invisible stairway that Duffy had gone down.

Duffy wondered if he should be afraid. Anyone who knew about the stairs in the sky must be intelligent and could be reasoned with, yes? Duffy stepped sideways and continued climbing on a different set of stairs. The cats remaining on the ground all formed a circle facing inward, glowing light touching golden light, the illumination spread out and engulfed Duffy and his body was burning with this light which jiggled every particle of his being. Duffy's toes curled and he shuddered, slipping from the invisible stair in the sky he tumbled into bed.

22

Duffy's head jerked up, the train car was dark, night had come. He looked around and saw the form of Starblaze in he bunk next to him, and the two others from the theater troupe occupying the other bunks and several on the floor as well. For safety from the killer on the loose and warmth from the night chill which was no longer conveniently heated. Tho the temperature at any time of year rarely dipped below fifty degrees, combined with the darkness and the killer, the sensation of a slight chill was magnified.

The landslide had knocked the rear of the train loose from the front and buried the opening to the tunnel, the train car which had been nearest the opening now lay far from the tracks, protruding from mud and boulders down the slope. All power from the engine units had been lost and the stranded rear of the train was dark and the network was down, there was no news feed on the walls, no communications systems, no lights, and doors had to be manually opened. Duffy's nose was bruised from walking into several doors which failed to open.

Duffy lay his head back down, wondering if he had done something to anger the gods and goddesses and genderless multi armed twelve eyed ancient entities, such as not believing in them, yes, that might have been where things went wrong. Duffy stared at the pattern on the ceiling, thinking about how his parents would never have gotten into a situation like this. Or had they simply suppressed the information of their personal struggles? Nothing to do now but be well rested for the morning. Duffy closed his eyes and worked on getting to sleep, which failed, so he got out of bed carefully stepping over snoring bodies into the hall where he leaned against the large round windows and stared out into the deep night. Stars in abundance, witness to the scene of human catastrophe. The stars had already seen it all so they made no mention or even dip in brightness to mark the moment. A small stack of bodies lay in a rearward car, locked in to keep them from the coyowolves and vultures so families might see their body one last time and perform rituals.

"Vacation of death, sunken ships and derailed trains, killers on the loose." Duffy mumbled to himself, how does a simple cafe owner go from an easy savory scone and herbal tea for breakfast to this wild extreme? In times like these people have always looked up to the mysterious sky for an answer and had reflected back at them what they wanted to believe, or what they suspected was true. A shooting star, yes, do I see the Answer now! A cloud passes over the moon, perhaps: Ask Again another night.

What Duffy received instead was an audible scream of terrifying sustain and pitch, the skin on the back of his neck tightened with electricity. When the sleepers in their berths came stumbling into the hall Duffy knew it was not his imagination.

"From this way!" Duffy said, and led the way, and exactly as he hoped, the passengers and crew followed as tho they had forgotten his association with the fugitive. At the first door they came to Duffy crashed into and a pile up of bodies formed behind him eliciting much cursing, "Sorry." Duffy said, and opened the door manually. The group searched car by car, all the survivors of the storm spilled into the hall in their jammies or naked or topless. A conductor with an Afro appeared and reached a dark skinned hand inside his coat to bring forth the new Manifest of the Rear which the survivors had composed before retiring the previous evening. This document was consented upon as a way of governing the situation while facing the reality being cut off from outside communications since the storm had damaged some essential regional communication infrastructure. Those in attendance gathered in the lounge car and called out their names one by one. All were accounted for.

"Then no one here is the source of the scream?" the conductor demanded and received nothing but silence.

"Perhaps it was the metal wreckage settling under the landslide." someone suggested. Others mumbled their hope that this was true, but Duffy looked left and right looking for a suspicious sign.

"The scream was human." a woman said.

The conductor pressed his hand to the face of the tablet containing the Manifest of the Rear and it's light went out. He placed the tablet deep inside a coat pocket over his heart, "Perhaps the killer has found justice among the wolves."

23

There was little sleep the remainder of the night, and none for Duffy. The moment his eyes slid shut he imagined the bright blue eyes of the fugitive and Duffy's tired eye lids would spring back open to a vision of nothing but the dark night.

In the morning Duffy and Starblaze went to the cafe car and finding the robo cook out of service they immediately decided on a trek to the other side of the mountain to see what had become of the head end of the train. No one else felt any enthusiasm about a wilderness hike after a night listening to the Coyowolves singing.

"We could send up a drone to look at the South end of the tunnel."

"There's a rack of drones on the engine unit, but none in the back." the conductor said.

"I've got a drone!" a young passenger volunteered, she ran and fetched it, unfolded the thing and set it down on the gravel ballast beside the tracks. The small black machine unfolded itself and with a slight whirring noise flew up and above the tree tops, higher still it went as the passengers watched the camera's view on a screen held by the young woman. Then a shadow moved over them as a massive golden eagle with claws extended crushed the drone in it's talons, everyone watching the screen jumped backwards, and the little machine spun down to crash in the forest. Starblaze and Duffy stood with their necks leaned back, taking in the whole scene. The young girl cursed and hung her head, "That was my birthday present."

"Someone on this train has angered spirits." a large man said, head leaned back watching the eagle circling above.

"Hard to argue with that." Starblaze said, "Things are rough. It's also migration season when raptors are flying south for the slightly chilly season and they don't like to cross large bodies of water because they cant float like a duck. No place to land out there if they're tired, so they follow the Gulf coast going South. Lot's of raptors on the coast this time of year, bad time to fly a small drone."

"That's a good argument." the large man said, "Beautiful beings, the eagles. Our drones are ugly."

Some of the crew were laboring to restore auxiliary power and the passengers decided to hold out for that, and for the hope of eventual rescue. Starblaze Sturgeon's troupe, normally so fond of a wild time, now fell prey to the fears of these unknown deep woods. This was no stage here, but the tall pine trees from which stages of old had been built, massive trees full of the stored energy of the sun, guarded by talons above and fangs below, trees kept warm by small brush fires that opened their cones and woke up life in the cells of the seeds.

As the two walked away from the train Starblaze inhaled the

fresh mountain air and smiled up to the sun, "Much better now! I can't stand loitering in proximity to dead bodies. Bad memories from childhood you know. I would prefer risking the unknown than stay on that death train."

"The storm has passed," Duffy said, "and coyowolves wont attack two people."

"So if one turns back, we both go back."

"And if one goes on, both go on."

"Agreed."

"And so was written the Manifest of Two Hikers."

They followed a muddy deer track that seemed to skirt the base of the mountain, slipping on soggy storm soil made for slow hiking, they struggled over many fallen branches and downed trees blocking the path.

"Coyowolf tracks." Starblaze said, pointing at the mud below, "One good thing about the mud."

"Is it?" Duffy stepped around the print and walked on. After many hours they emerged into a small clearing where groups of birch trees grew along a small stream flowing off the mountain. They paused and took rest on several dry boulders while the sun shone down, warming their deep woods chilled toes.

"Do you hear that?" Duffy asked.

Starblaze listened, "The buzzing? You've never heard that sound?"

"No, have you?"

"Come listen." Starblaze took his hand and he followed Starblaze to a stand of birch trees, "Put your ear on the bark."

Duffy followed her direction and placed an ear on the tree, the buzzing noise became so loud he almost jumped back.

"It's a termite, once confined to certain parts of the world by other insect predators and by harsh zones of deep winter. Nothing to hold them back now. We may be the last generation to see a wild birch tree. Welcome to the dawning of the Age of Insects. It kinda overlaps the Anthropocene."

"It's my favorite smell, birch wood burning. And even this goes."

"We shouldn't let them go."

Duffy stood with his hand on the tree, looking around at the many white birch trunks and feeling the life of the forest, "How can we hold on? It feels like a struggle to hold our own lives."

"We are much like these trees, aren't we." Starblaze put her ear to the birch tree and closed her eyes.

They walked on. Further around the mountain they arrived at an overlook where the sky and valley beyond lay open to see, remains of the weather system that produced the hurricane floated in long wispy strips across the sky. A tall snag of a white pine tree stood still majestic even in it's charred lightning strike wooden skeleton, near the top a massive golden eagle sat on a barren branch, relaxed in solitude.

Starblaze and Duffy stood on the precipice for a long time, silent.

"We better make the tunnel before dark." Starblaze said, and the golden eagle's head turned toward them before unfolding graceful wings and dancing across the valley and out of sight. Starblaze and Duffy continued back into the forest on criss-crossing deer trails around the mountain.

The sun was at their back now in the afternoon when the trail broke out of dense undergrowth, ahead they could see a glimpse of the gulf waters stretching to a far horizon.

"We're a long way off I know, but it feels good to see it. At least we know there is another side!" Duffy held out his arms and twisted, cracking his back, and shook his limbs trying to catch a second wind.

"Keep going?" Starblaze Sturgeon smiled.

Soon the trail disappeared onto solid rock and they stood at an overlook with light green lichens and vibrant green moss, below train tracks wound south thru forested hills.

"Worse case scenario: we walk back to New Bear. How far are we?"

Duffy looked at the Southern horizon, "The remainder of the summer I think. Have you ever walked on railroad tracks? It's awkward. Some ties are close together, then some far apart, they designed walking on the tracks to be annoying to keep people from walking on them. Engineers expressing such a delicate love of life. Meanwhile the trains carried loads of carbon to burn and bring on climate change."

"Six million years of evolution and we let it slip from our hands, now we trust engineer's equations to keep us alive. Woops, and sometimes they miss the big picture."

"Conscious adaptation. There is no more evolution! We've taken over the controls, thus the Anthropocene."

"The learning curve went straight down."

The descent to the train tracks was rapid, soon they were struggling to walk on the ties, awkwardly advancing towards the tunnel. Arriving at the cliff base they saw no train but only a round mouth of darkness.

"Could be in there still. Pretty long tunnel." Starblaze said.

"Let's find out." Duffy took his pack off and got a lamp out and clipped it on, "I'll leave my pack here in case a rescue party comes so they will see it and know we are in there."

"Good idea Duffy."

Starblaze and Duffy walked into the tunnel and followed the gleam from Duffy's light on the polished steel of the rails stretching far into darkness. The sound of four feet walking was all they heard for an hour and then they stopped walking and stared at a wall of jumbled rock and trees illuminated by Duffy's lamp.

"That's it. They left us. They probably had a lot of critically wounded people needing hospital." Starblaze said.

Duffy felt a wave of ill feeling sweep over and his old suspicions of Starblaze all came back, for just a moment and then it was gone, but in that moment his presence changed, a door opened and he saw a myriad of possible futures, some of which he wished to avoid, some which he seemed attracted to. Futures he wished to avoid were ones that included the refugee killer and Starblaze in a conspiracy to commit some crime involving Duffy, such as identity theft involving murder or something else, what it was he could not imagine. Why would someone do that to a poor service industry worker? It was a hard concept to conceive but Duffy tried and unfortunately came to several conclusions that were undesirable as he debated himself, "Could these come true or are they only bad waking dreams, and if it was real dreams that brought Starblaze and I together then how can you tell what dreams are real and what is consciousness, what memories real and what fantasy, our minds working hard to keep us alive and safe, our minds taking the raw data from our senses and mixing it together to make a tasty cake and we happily eat the cake but is it the truth? No, the truth is too brutal, it would stir our emotions so much it could kill us, so we never stare at the full harsh light, we do not eat the cake raw, and even fully baked we still demand frosting."

"Let's head back to the mouth," Duffy said aloud, "if we're lucky a rescue train will be there soon."

"Hmmm." Starblaze said, "Very optimistic."

The walk back was much quieter, Duffy contemplated every sound and scanned his light left and right, illuminating the entire tunnel so no blue eyed murderer could be lurking against the damp rock walls after following them into their death trap. Duffy's light began to dim and he turned it off to save what power remained, holding the device in his hand at the ready.

"Oo! What's that?" Starblaze froze, and Duffy thot the moment had come for their screams to ring out and never be heard again.

"Light!" Starblaze pointed to the end of the tunnel and a sensation of light so faint it might be a hallucination.

"Can you see me?" Starblaze said.

Duffy saw the faintest outline of a person next to him, "Yes!"

Starblaze took two steps to meet Duffy and embraced him with a kiss. Duffy's heart was pounding in fear. Starblaze smiled, "Are you afraid of the dark?"

"It makes me imagine unpleasant possibilities. Yes."

"Now you can remember this moment when there was nothing to fear. Let's go!" Starblaze took his hand and they walked into the increasing brightness.

"Duffy!" Starblaze whispered as they arrived at the mouth of the cave, "Cute!" she pointed at a large rabbit near the tracks, sniffing inside Duffy's small pack that he had left there.

"I forgot there was food in there!"

"City slick." Starblaze smiled.

The bunny looked around while chewing then dove back in for another root and a great snowy owl appeared on top of the rabbit, long feathered legs with talons grabbed the entire scene and working it's great white and black barred wings the owl flew away with it all.

Duffy ran out of the tunnel entrance and looked into the sky, hoping his pack might fall and be recovered, "That just happened. I have nothing but the clothes on my back."

Starblaze was silent while Duffy walked to the spot where his bag had been and found only some drops of fresh blood and an empty food wrapper.

"I wouldn't read too much into this. They don't call it the wilderness for nothing." Starblaze said, "Tell me Duffy. Do you ever listen to what the spirits say?"

24

Duffy stared into a sky that had three slightly different colored suns, yet somehow it did not seem too bright, only very deep and rich in hue and glow. Difficult to avoid looking directly at the sun when there were three of them in the sky. Duffy closed his eyes and the suns spun rapidly in the darkness of the space behind his eyelids, rapidly following orbits in a dance of gravity, the largest sun only wobbling slightly in a shy two-step. A star is a thing of joy and universal warmth, Duffy smiled and when he opened his eyes he saw the grass was deep and thick where he lay and next to him was Starblaze.

"How did you get here?" Duffy asked her.

"Don't you know?"

Duffy stood up, the seed heads of the grass barely below his chin, he could see the edge of the meadow where the forest began and a darkness inside, a vigorous forest, canopy full of leaves allowing no light for the understory, ripe for a fire or tornado or insect destruction to open the crown up and let the three suns warm the fertile soil full of endless life. Deep in Light Forest the birds danced across the tops of the trees chasing swarms of insects cavorting in their own dance, down below trod a weary toad and turtle, Pagnellopy and Xippix paused a moment near a cluster of spice leaf trees.

"Do you think we should stay on the path?" Pagnellopy looked out into the inviting forest.

"Without the path, how do we know which way to go? Also, the path is faster. I do not want a stick in the eye."

"That's reasonable. Just checking the options."

"I am hungry. Should we split another fish?" Xippix stretched out turtle arms in a luxurious way, "I could eat a whole one myself."

"No. Xippix. We've already eaten half of what we brought for the cats."

"Hmm. We can catch more on the way. I'm good at fishing."

"I think we might be lucky to find a couple Crawlingfish under some rocks, back in these woods. That would make small gift for the cats."

"How much further is Light Hollow, oh right, not supposed to ask anymore. Hey, do I see water up there? There's a lake, maybe fishing, or we can just swim! Funny how a hot day just makes you wanna dive in no matter what else is going on."

"The journey is the destination. Here we are. Gotta keep living while doing good work."

The two strolled lively up to the bright open air and the clear waters of the mountain lake.

"This is luscious!" Xippix said and threw pack on the ground to scamper in the water and dive down, emerging further out turtle head emerged and mouth breathed air and Xippix floated there with internal air pockets under the hard back shell.

"It's very nice. I can smell so much in the water, we can fish for sure."

After half and hour Xippix crawled out of the lake on all fours, exhausted form swimming after fish and reduced to an older evolutionary stage.

"Water is too clean, they saw me coming."

"Buddy. Sit on the grass. We have a long way to hike yet today."

Xippix groaned, "City life has done me wrong. I've lost my survival skills."

"Yeah, turtles invented fishing nets for a reason, just like toads invented insect traps, instead of spending all our energy to get food we spend a little energy to get food and a lot of energy to expand our brains and extend our social connections. Life is so much easier when shared."

"I'm no primitive that's true." Xippix said, "When I graduate I want to go into fish farming. I love fish. I mean, why wouldn't you?"

The two continued on the path which wrapped around the lake and continued into the woods. It was much later when only one sun was in the sky of Gaeiou during crimson hour that Pagnellopy heard the noise behind them and turned to catch sight of a shadow that moved between tree trunks. Too tall to be a small forest creature, it was two legged and big, but no horns, it wasn't a Rochie. An indigenous forest toad? A few tribes still did exist out in the wild depths of Light Forest, protected by law. Or might someone have followed them up from the market to rob them? A strange thot but there was an increasing amount chaos in the world these days.

Pagnellopy touched Xippix's arm and motioned silence. They stood listening and heard a twig snap.

Pagnellopy whispered, "Should we hide and wait for the person to pass and see who it is?"

"Let's turn back and confront them!" Xippix insisted.

"No, that plays into their strength, they could see us coming and ambush us. We should find a place to hide so we can watch them pass by. Then we can decide if we want to engage them or not!"

"Acquiescence."

Pagnellopy and Xippix walked on until a small crop of rock covered with a dwarf forest above presented itself, they quietly crept into the hilltop and lay still in the thick growth. Pagnellopy meditated in the silence. When one listens to the world, really stops and listens mindfully to every sound, even the quiet places are very loud. A forest contains wind touching green leaves, branches clacking together, brown dry leaves on the ground rub on each other like drum heads, birds sing chirp and squawk, insects so tasty and crunchy being eaten, small warm blooded beasts thrash thru the underbrush, water trickles in streams and from trees, even dead branches can snap off and go tumbling to the ground like cymbals crashing. Other sounds, unidentified, all forming a singular melody.

For a long time Pagnellopy and Xippix listened to these sounds, crouched unmoving in the bush, wondering if the person following them had a thermographic lens to see their heat signatures and wishing they had a micro bird to send up and fly the perimeter so they might see a preview of the approaching figure. They had only awareness and time, every few minutes the remaining fish tucked safe in their packs would whip tail and make a tiny noise. Xippix made a silent biting chewing motion while pointing at the packs and Pagnellopy replied with a silent four eyed scowl and negative shake of warty young toad jowls.

The shadow was visible now, someone was coming up the trail, Pagnellopy tensed and then focused on control of toad scent glands, a technique that Grandstar had taught. If the person approaching was another toad they would smell the distress pheromones and be alerted to the presence of another toad.

It was a toad! Pagnellopy watched carefully, the loping gait of this young but muscular toad wearing the jacket of Pagnellopy's own school. Pagnellopy felt a chill, it was Chartles!

Xippix' hands slowly clenched and Pagnellopy quietly moved their arm close to Xippix to hold those angry turtle fists. They watched in unmoving silence as Chartles skulked up the path, glancing right and left, passed by, and disappeared into the woods beyond.

"That racist bully." Xippix whispered, "Chartles is not here for a fun nature hike. Now what?"

"We follow. Or go back the way we came. Your opinion?"

"We could also continue sitting here. Or we could go that way!" Xippix pointed away from the trail, "Or we could call your sibling and have them fly us outta here. I heard them offer, you know they're just waiting for a call. People are so afraid of the woods, you would think we never even came from here."

"That is only if we are in serious trouble, it really is quite offensive to fly into Light Forest and would compromise our goals in coming here. The cats will never help us if we do that."

"What did you think of the look that was on Chartles face?" Xippix said.

"Angry and focused."

"Possibly armed."

"Chartles is a horrible bully but I don't think a murderer. There are two of us, I don't think he would try anything."

"Pagnellopy, what does bullying look like out in the woods where there are no witnesses and little possibility of being held accountable? After going thru all this trouble to find us, all by himself, I don't think he's going to use rough language, I think it might involve extreme violence."

Pagnellopy stared into the woods were Chartles had gone, "I don't want to believe it. I know from rumors that something terrible happened to him deep in the past, I mean, no one is born like that, but now it seems something has happened recently that made this toad snap."

"This is so weird. I'm scared." Xippix put their hand in Pagnellopy's and held it.

A wind moved slowly thru the forest, causing a few leaves to fall from the tall trees, Pagnellopy watched the movement with alert eyes, "Maybe Chartles just wants to come apologize like Wixha."

"Mmm." Xippix let his eyes move across the horizon of the forest, "No. Chartles knows what we're doing and is trying to stop us. He walks with a narrow vision, in righteous anger, and has decided that we are the enemy. Chartles is not one of us."

25

Duffy opened his eyes, a shaft of light shone thru the glass brick window high up the concrete wall of the rail service shack. The companions had found their way in thru a ventilation duct on the roof and slept out of the wind in the darkness. Now that morning had come it was time to explore the resources of the rail shack without bumbling into sharp metal and dangerous high voltage electronics powered by the large solar panels on the roof.

Duffy smiled at the sun coming thru the window, any day the sun was out was a day that had at least one good thing going. Starblaze awoke as Duffy stirred and they unfolded themselves from a cozy sleeping pretzel of arms and legs. The shack was long and contained several electric powered maintenance vehicles parked on the tracks along with stacks of sealed crates and numerous miscellaneous objects. Duffy crawled into a cab of one vehicle and found a cache of sealed water bottles which he shared with Starblaze and they enjoyed a breakfast of water.

Starblaze picked up a phone button from the dash board and tried to make a call, "Dead. That storm really laid out some towers." Starblaze patted the dashboard of the rail car, "This is looking hopeful. You think can we hot wire one of these jobs and head out?"

"This aint no robo chef. I can see what about it. I learned a bit from my mother, she was good with complicated systems. My dad, he was more of a sculptor really. He could make it work and look good. My mom could figure out how it was even possible."

"Sounds like a good mix. You were close to them?"

"I was fortunate to be close to them. Lot of families didn't even make it thru the Reformation."

"My parents went South." Starblaze said, "Back to the homeland, Argentina. Last I heard. Long way to travel on the holidays."

"When's the last time you saw them?"

"Years."

"Long way to Argentina."

"That's the world we live in."

Duffy stepped up to the cab of the lead car and slid the orange door open, squinted at the control panel. A light flashed indicating a trickle charge from the shack's solar panels. Duffy climbed down and rooted thru the tool boxes until he found a writer/reader that looked operational and plugged it into the control panel. Soon he had bypassed the key lock and started the computer.

"Batteries are full charged."

"I got the door!" Starblaze worked the buttons, the massive bolt lock slid back and the doors swung slowly open to a blast of daylight and Starblaze howled with her fists in the air. Duffy engaged the drive and the electric turbines sang, he rolled the car slowly out the shack and Starblaze jumped up on the fly and they rolled on South without looking back. To the right were gentle hills alternating with steep bluffs, on the left the warm waters of the Gulf.

The rail car whirred a low, comforting rumble as the engines ran into the sunny day, Starblaze worked at the screen to see if the local track grid was functioning, "It would be a tragedy to be run over by one's own rescue train!" The forest whizzed by, the tracks cutting thru small hills, rolling past abandoned wooden houses on hilltops rotten and slumped with broken out windows looking like the skulls of giants.

"What did you do before owning the Far North?"

Duffy pulled his eyes away from the hypnotically scrolling landscapes and leaned back in the comfortable seat, "I rambled for years. Rolled in the bushes drunk. Put my arms around anything that would keep me from flying off the world. It spun faster back then, I swear. Slept on cardboard in windowless buildings below the nests of winged creatures. Lived in homes I built on the outskirts, shacks in the construction slums of Northern cities like New Bear, surfing on the high density boom. I look back and wonder how much of my life was wasted, but it was fun, mostly, what I remember. I survived with the ability to be happy now, which is what I must have been trying to do then, since here I am. I worked in the warehouse at New Bear when it was established, five years and they called it done. Brutal architecture. Hideous. I call that concrete home. Radiation and hurricane proof. It was pretty exciting to move out of the tents." Duffy looked out on the horizon as it undulated while the rail car cruised, "You need a thick skin in this world. Hard not to feel weird, when the refugees were massing on our Southern border and we just shrugged and kept working, happy we were in the sweet spot. Now I wonder when I hear about the other cities being built, and how New World Gulf might become unlivable from the spring hurricanes. We can't just live inside a bunker for months on end. Or maybe we can. Maybe in a few years we find ourselves massing on someone's border, on the wrong side. Ho, look at that!" Duffy pointed out the curved front window of the rail car at several deer moving alongside the tracks, "I hope the wildlife-scatter program is working on this thing."

"More of your folks in you. These technical skills. It all started with them, ya? Funny how people end up being a part of us and we don't really get to choose, people do what they do, we experience what they do, and then we process that and it becomes part of us. Doesn't matter if we want it or not. You had old school mom and dad parents. I grew up in a farming collective. God based."

"A cult?"

"Yeah, pretty far out. Faith based activities. Making stuff up without any scientific reality check at all. I mean, that's kinda fun, creative. But not even a scientific theory behind it. How hard is it to come up with a theory? That's creative too. Science is all about faith, when you get into the deep physics, I cant do that math, I just have to believe that those who can do math are telling what they believe to be the truth. And then about the time I decided the way I was raised was a bunch of lies, climate change hit the top of the hill and started heading down. No brakes! Didn't matter if it was human caused or a natural cycle, the ice was gone by the time I turned twenty. A generation, just like that. I see children and I wonder why they don't ask about it, they're not even sad. They've never seen snow. They don't even know it's gone. It's better that way I guess. When they're a little older and getting deeper into learning, you can see the joy goes away, when they know. It's hard to see the transition out of innocence, the anger at older generations. It's sad." Starblaze turned and looked out the window as a green blur of forest went by, "Life adapts. You wonder if we're gonna make it, nothing lasts forever, so many extinctions, and we may go soon, in a blink of geologic time. Scientists say we can make it, but do we really have faith in that vision?"

Duffy stretched, "We better figure it out cause we can't even leave the planet yet. One life one planet. Do or die. We're on the run, and there's not much more North to run to. Then what, go under water? Underground? Back to the caves? Devolution."

"Half the world population is gone so there's a huge drop in emissions, but now the feedback loops are in full effect. We cant wait around for the Earth to heal itself when we are the ones who knocked it down. We have to do the healing. We better push the right button this time."

The storm system that brought a hurricane two days ago seemed to have pulled all the clouds along when it left, there was only the sun in the sky. The micro solar collector skin of the rail car charged the batteries as they rolled on hour after hour. Scenes of wild invasive plant growth flew by and the ripples on the gulf waters sparkled like nothing bad had ever happened.

The rail car lurched and entered automatic slowdown. On the tracks ahead a human figure waved their arms overhead. The rail car came to a full stop as Duffy and Starblaze stared at the figure.

"What am I looking at here?" Duffy asked.

"Looks like a damn Viking." Starblaze said.

The pale skinned person standing on the tracks was clad in buckskin and wore a fur hat, they suddenly lowered their hands and bent over in a violent cough.

"Aw damn. They got the Global Pneumonie. We better find some masks in the med kit." Starblaze rummaged in a locker behind the seats and found two bio hazard masks and synthetic gloves. They put on the gear then pushed the door open and stepped out of the car. The woman approached with arms up and palms out, "There's been a terrible storm, we need help!"

"What's wrong with you, the coughing?" Starblaze touched the elbow of the refugee woman with her gloved hand.

"What does it look like? I'm not here to get help for myself, there are many people that need help more than me. Can you help?"

There's a doctor on the rail car, let me get it." Duffy went back and unlocked the robo doc and carried it with them as they followed the woman down a trail to the survivors. As they left, the rail car went into safety mode and dropped four wheels down to move itself off the mainline track. Starblaze and Duffy followed the stranger for ten minutes, climbing over numerous blown down trees. Something emerged from the destroyed undergrowth as they passed, a small child with light brown skin and many tears. Duffy picked the young human up and tiny arms encircled his neck.

"What's your name?"

"My name is Ruth."

"Where are you going?"

"I'm looking for you!"

Duffy did not ask anymore questions and Ruth joined them on the trail. As they continued walking sounds of anguish revealed their arrival at the destroyed refugee camp. Fallen trees lay everywhere, tents, tarps, and possessions were strewn everywhere on the ground and up in the branches of trees. Groups of children huddled together comforted by aunties, uncles, and grandmas. Random dogs wandered thru the remains, no longer fastidiously guarding the perimeter but confused about the new order, processing what had happened and checking on loved ones and also wondering about supper. Duffy approached a group of children and put Ruth down, the elder welcomed the storm child into her arms. On the other side of the small village meadow two men dug with hand tools at the rocky ground where a man was trapped under a massive pine tree.

Duffy put the robo doc on the ground and pressed the activating sequence. The silver case unfolded itself and stood up as a two meter high matte silver humanoid.

"Active. Ready." the robot said.

"Triage: one hundred meters approximate radius."

"What happened here?" the robot asked.

"Hurricane."

The robo doc moved out at a trot, rapidly scanning the entire area and then moved thru a second time administering painkiller to several people who were vocalizing their suffering. The robo doc returned to Duffy, "Recommend activating twelve additional robotic doctors."

"You're the only robo doc, sorry."

The doctor got to work on the most urgent cases from the dozens of patients laid out across the meadow. Duffy and Starblaze helped the people who were digging out the trapped man. Duffy paused to look around, the refugees may have all been illegals. Living conditions in the camp seemed primitive but functional. They were hunting and gathering, wearing deer skins decently tanned and fashioned, someone must have taught them this skill. There were large vegetable gardens under fallen branches, it looked like a decent life may have been lived before the hurricane struck, unknown in the wilderness without proper documentation, they were safe from the authorities, and perhaps befriended by old school traditional native tribes that amalgamated here during the Northern Migration and lived in the deep woods paddling canoes on forgotten streams. Those tribes would not dwell so close to the gulf, they knew the dangers.

"Why do you live so close to the Gulf?" Starblaze asked an elder.

"We fish the gulf, our boats hidden on the shore. We thot this would be a safe camp, it is a long walk to the shore! We must change our ways, build stronger houses, learn the ways of the gulf sky. I was born a long way from here. This place frightens me."

"I live in a house made of stone, and sometimes I am afraid." Duffy said.

The refugees were of all kinds, a community of necessity, their skins not just the white of the woman on the tracks but many colors and their bodies many shapes, jewelry and tattoos and various garments showed no dominant culture except for the local deer hides they wore as coats and pants and fresh woven grass hats to shield from the sun.

The man under the log was pulled out under supervision of the robo doc who then deployed a sterile field pressure bag over his legs and preformed surgery so that he might walk again.

Some of the leaders rallied the survivors to assemble a roof from the remains of the least destroyed house made of logs and tarps so they could shelter the wounded. Starblaze and Duffy joined the children harvesting dead dry sticks from the trunks of pine and spruce trees to make a comforting fire near the refurbished shelter. The robo doc made a report and Duffy and Starblaze walked back to the rail car to fetch a fresh battery pack. The robo doc would need to work on the wounded all day and into the night. They switched the battery out 3 times before sunset and Duffy was happy the day had been sunny and the solar cells had kept the batteries in the rail car ready to go.

The refugees gathered what food they had found after being scattered by the hurricane and shared food with the survivors around the fire. Duffy and Starblaze refused, still wearing their masks and gloves, noticing several at the fire pause during eating to cough deeply. Feeling the hunger and thirst, Starblaze and Duffy returned to the rail car to drink and eat rations from the lockers.

"There's a part of me that wants to fire this thing up right now and get out of here." Duffy said, "A mask and gloves feel like thin protection against the G-Pneumonie. I don't want to see anymore death. Also, I'm homesick."

Outside the windows of the rail car a wind blew in the darkness and rocked the car on it's suspension, "I worked for years there in New Bear, never thot I would leave. Why would I? And then everything changed and here I am."

"Choices." Starblaze said, "I made many small decisions that brought me to this place, but I didn't choose to come here specifically. I made choices and here I am. So I did choose this but I didn't really know what I was choosing. Such mystery in life. I love it. You know why I love it? Cause I don't want it to go away."

A knock sounded on the door of the rail car and Duffy opened it. From the dark several faces moved into the light, "We want to leave this place. Our immune systems are strong but we fear the sickness. Let us come with you." A small child's face appeared in the doorway, it was Ruth. The woman who spoke picked Ruth up and placed her inside the rail car.

26

Duffy felt his breathing become slow and regular along with the wheels of the rail car rolling on the steel rails, then the wheels went to sleep and the car rose gently off the steel tracks, the sound of air caressing the aerodynamic lozenge of the rail car as it soared like Apollo 18 directly into space. Duffy twitched as it first separated from the tracks, like falling out of bed while asleep but you don't really fall out of bed you just twitch and groan and go back to sleep and find yourself safely back on the thick grass of another planet walking away from the metal cocoon made on Earth. The rail car lay upside down at the end of a smoking gouge in the ground, wheels spinning slightly, catching light on their polished curved bottoms. A successful landing.

With each footstep the grass parted in front of Duffy until he entered the dark woods beyond the field and found the trail he was attracted to. The darkness smelled alive. Duffy became aware that he was surrounded by numerous lights that accompanied him as he walked. For sure he knew them, beings of light, they moved with him thru the forest until he could no longer feel his feet touching the ground and no tree branches touched his hands or face. Duffy moved fluidly thru the air, he was one of the lights. Ahead the forest grew brighter and another meadow with golden grass spread out beyond, at the tree line on the opposite side stood a toad and turtle.

Pagnellopy and Xippix stepped cautiously into the meadow, having taken the longer path around they hoped Chartles would believe they were lost and turn back, but if Chartles continued on, could that toad be in Light Hollow to meet them? What would the cats do? Were they gone? Had they destroyed Chartles and were they angry at the lowlanders? They must be aware of visitors in the wood, the toad and turtle who walked in Light Hollow.

Duffy floated and arrived at the center of the meadow simultaneously with the toad and turtle where a boulder rose above the highest seed heads of the tallest grasses. Under that boulder lay many big cats catching rays from the suns, stretching as they heard the grass shuffling. Several cat heads could be seen above the grass, curiously looking at the toad and turtle approaching.

"Oh they really are huge!" Pagnellopy said, "As tall as us!"

"Yes. Looks like they are waking up from a nap. I'm always so hungry after a nap." Xippix gripped their pack straps.

"Let's not hesitate on the fringe," Pagnellopy said, "In we go!"

The most awake and alert cat stretched and sprang to the top of the boulder and sat fully upright, shades of dark yellow striping fur with a bold swath of white emblazoning the ruff that puffed out from the cat's chest while slow blinking at the bright light of wakefulness. The cat turned it's gaze to Pagnellopy and Xippix and the head of the creature began to glow.

"Meow." the cat said to them but the whiskered mouth did not move.

"Thank you." Pagnellopy said, "We have come here without knowing how your day is going and we hope you accept our arrival."

"You are welcome."

"My name is Pagnellopy."

"My name is Xippix."

"Yes, you tell the truth." the cat yawned wildly, "My name will remain secret. Now, I smell a snack and I wonder if you have something to share with us, having traveled from the place of magic where endless snacks lay stacked and stored in portable ponds made of wood loaded with fish of all flavors. We get so hungry when compelled to perform favors for the whole of Gaeiou. It's quite a responsibility."

"Yes, oh, we have what we could carry. A slight gift, as much as two young students might be expected to manage." Xippix laughed and took off turtle pack and setting it on the ground carefully took out the sack of fish. Pagnellopy did the same. The entire gathering of big cats had silently risen and was moving towards them. Black striped cats, yellow striped cats, white cats, brown cats, black cats, spotted cats and mottled cats, they now silently circled Pagnellopy and Xippix, slowly savoring what smells pulled them forward.

"As I count heads now I fear we may not have enuf for everyone." Xippix said, "Would it be rude to suggest that the fish might be shared equally in some way? Or, we would be happy to fetch more fish and simply return this time tomorrow."

"This could be the first of many gifts." Pagnellopy looked sadly down into the half full sack of fish.

"Mmmm, tempting." the yellow striped cat's head radiated golden streamers of light, "Waiting for future pleasure takes away from our enjoyment of the present moment. Also, we have our own accounting. We take turns feasting. You stand under fortunate suns."

The cat yawned, exposing enormous fangs and many other sharp teeth, then jumped down from the rock, "Me first."

Pagnellopy opened the bag and drained the water, then taking one by the tail Pagnellopy placed it in the cat's opened mouth who returned to their rock and ate the morsel while the rest of the cats moved in their secret order to accept their gift while some watched curiously at a distance.

"We have seen you in dreams." the cat said, more relaxed now, "We have also seen other spirits who are not from this world, but they are strangely connected to you."

A long haired white cat next to Xippix spoke, "We see them walking on the sky."

And a short haired black cat next to Pagnellopy, "They have the glow. They have affinity with you."

A calico whispered, "They are watching."

"They are here now." the yellow cat looked beyond the circle, out at the grass of the meadow.

As the cats looked his way Duffy turned and looked behind himself, frightened, before realizing they were talking about him.

Pagnellopy and Xippix spun toad heads around looking.

"It is unlikely you will see them." the cat on the rock said.

A scraggly looking orange short hair cat stepped forward, "Speak aloud the reason you have come to us?"

"We want to help life on Gaeiou. Toads and turtles have been selfish and have damaged the environment. We want to bring the balance back."

"The warm days have grown shorter." The cat on the boulder said, "I do not like this."

"I love to play in the snow." a gray black striped cat said, "But I do not want to play in the snow every day."

"A terrible storm is coming that we cannot survive." the white longhair said, "How do you want us to help you? We also help ourselves."

"We want to share the story of what happened in Heart City with all of Gaeiou, we had success but we think it must spread across the planet and find a home in the hearts of all toads and turtles to be truly successful. We all share the same sky and we want to inspire toads and turtles everywhere to believe that we can be planetary citizens. One love. One world."

"Ripples in the water." the calico said.

The scraggly orange cat glowed, "As when three suns match magnetic field cycles and peak, then snap! Solar flares send the rainbows thru our minds."

"Revolution." the black cat's golden aura pulsed.

"We can do this." the yellow cat on the boulder said, "Are you prepared to open yourself and share all that has led to this, your failures and shame? Be prepared. You cannot hold back once it is begun, and you cannot take it back once it has been shared."

"We are ready." Pagnellopy said.

"No regrets." Xippix said.

"Come up here."

Pagnellopy sprang to the top of the boulder on toad legs and Xippix clambered after. The yellow cat dropped down to join the other cats who circled the boulder until each was equally spaced, then they sat on their haunches with front legs fully straight and chest out, eyes forward fully awake in the mindful position. Their heads began radiating a golden light that enveloped first the circle of cats, then the boulder, then the entire meadow. Pagnellopy felt the glands on the back of toad neck tingle and felt a warm glow of light come up from the center of Gaeiou, thru the grass, toad feet, legs, body, head, and out the top to spread across the world and into the universe beyond.

27

The sun rose without an audible noise but with a rumble so low that a human ear could not perceive the sound, it could be felt inside the body, on what might be called the electro magnetic spiritual level of consciousness. Duffy awoke to see brilliant red streaks on the bellies of clouds under the sky of morning. The waters of the Gulf crashed in small waves on the rocks that made up the rough young shoreline of peak global ice melt. Laying hidden in the grass above the beach Starblaze and the refugees slept. The railroad was a few kilometers West, the rail car abandoned when a train from the South came on the grid map. Duffy felt unsettled about the decision. This would not go well if the authorities in New Bear found out, but the refugees did not want to be deported back into the scald lands, back to the Re-United States where there would be little possibility of joy. The box cities were brutal conditions for the poor and the dome cities too expensive for a poor person unless allowed entry as a service worker, a life spent chained in the basement under a relative paradise was no life. Between them and the tracks lay kilometers of ugly jungle, the Kudzu had raced North every day for a hundred years and easily matched the pace of the warming climate, even the insect hordes found the vine too toxic and difficult to chew.

They carried everything useful from the rail car and waited now for a ship that would take them South, the captain was a friend of Starblaze Sturgeon. Duffy could not sleep but sat watching the sunrise while holding his head in his hands. There was no tea, coffee, toast, jam, or butter in this place. "I like to relax after a busy day by siting in a comfortable chair and watching my cat lick it's fur." Duffy said to the ocean, "We are far away from that."

Starblaze turned her head, "Did you say something?"

Duffy twitched his head as tho bit by an insect.

Starblaze sat up and woke the rest of the refugees to prepare for the day. She learned each of the refugee's names and asked them questions until there was an understanding between everyone. Duffy admired her skills, the limited communications necessary for painting roofs and food service work had not polished his people skills. Duffy was more a right-hemisphere brain person: singing was much easier than speaking language.

The color in the sky deepened as Duffy sat up and stretched, hungry but happy to be in this quiet and beautiful place. The horizon showed no ship as yet, the synthetic sails of a converted diesel freighter would be hard to miss.

When the sky lost all it's hues of red and pink and only blue sky and white clouds remained, one of the refugees pointed at the water horizon and there they saw the small dot of a ship. Two hours later, perhaps blown by a good east wind, the slow freighter was close enuf for those on land to see people moving on it's steel deck.

Starblaze spoke on her phone to the ship, soon a small boat could be seen throwing up white spray as it motored toward them.

"Have you had that phone the whole time?" Duffy said.

"I don't like to use it much. Emergencies only." Starblaze held her open hand out to the Gulf, "Can't walk on water. Get out much?"

"I'm sure this entire adventure makes up for it."

Soon the boat slid up on a flat area of the beach and a spry Black woman wearing thick brown pants and a blue plaid shirt with weather blown salty hair held back in a hot pink ribbon jumped from the bow of the boat to dry ground, "Starblaze Sturgeon!" she stepped up and embraced Starblaze laughing and kissed each cheek, "This is my man here, Karpay Lee."

"Fine to meet you at last." Starblaze embraced the muscular sailor who had no visible tattoos but wore a pair of sunglasses held in a brilliant frame woven from many small golden wires all entwined. Starblaze kissed each of his cheeks, then stepped back to make introductions, "Captain Margerite, this is Duffy, and here is David, John, Abe, Sam, Sarah, Mary, and young Ruth."

"Oi, traveling with the apostles." Karpay Lee said.

"The Merry Gentleman accepts all who request assistance." Captain Margerite said, "Please be welcome aboard."

Captain Margerite and her man Karpay Lee helped the refugees onto the skiff followed by Starblaze, Duffy brought up the back of the line, "Will we all fit?"

Starblaze turned around and helped Duffy onto the skiff, "A little tight."

Shoulder to shoulder they bounced against the waves rolling in from across the Gulf. Duffy felt his spine compact with each jolt and found a throw-able life preserver to sit on.

Starblaze glanced at Duffy, "Much better, thanks."

The refugees smiled and most of them did the same, finding floatation vests under the seats they sat on them and their previous expressions of anxiety lessened.

"During the windmill boom I owned a food truck down in Duluth and we would take a sailboat out on lake Gitchi Gami, up the Minnesota shore, the wind was better for sailing that way. I much prefer sailing to motoring, this brutalization of the water." Duffy frowned as spray from a hull beaten wave rained over everyone sitting in the front of the boat.

"Did you own the sailboat?"

"No, fans of my cello playing, they convinced me to bring the instrument out on the boat. I had a synthetic one that was somewhat waterproof so it worked out. The deck of a sailboat is an inspiring and challenging place to play cello."

"Jameson didn't tell me you played cello. Do you still play?"

"Yes. My cellos are back at home." Duffy looked away from her eyes.

"Home! Yes. I hope Mandelai is watering my plants." Starblaze smiled, "Seems like every time I go on tour I loose one and I'm very fond of them. But do you play out for other people or only alone? I would like it if you scored a performance with us in the holler."

Duffy smiled, "I might. When I started playing I imagined it would be my job, I would just play cello and people would love it and I would be rich. Funny how you get fantastic ideas in your head when young and it truly seems possible. I wanted to make music and live free."

"But you did not live the dream."

"I gave up on the money and just played for free, free cello in the streets! For tips, enuf for food to eat, people liked it. I was the guy who played cello in the street. Then I woke up one day needing money, a lot of money, and I thot, I've spent all my life trying to become a good cello player, why haven't I been paid for this? Not rich, no, not wealthy, enuf to get by, but by then I had become known as the guy who played cello for free in the streets and I didn't even know how to sell myself and it felt like the world had passed me by, danced away on the melody from my instrument and taken their wallets with them. I was making some money selling food to workers out of my truck so I drove it North with the emigration allotment and the United Tribes allowed me into the Cafe Circle. On some nights I set up in the dining room and wear a mask of feathers and I play. I don't think they know its me. Most people hardly know I exist, the robo servers are the ones doing all the customer service. I'm the man behind the curtain, and that can be fun when it's not lonely. It's a privilege to live in the North, able to walk outside any time of day, safe from the sun, safe from crime, for now, a decade from today our homes may all be abandoned, nothing left but dusty footprints in a desert. This is the world we live in."

"A world we inherited." Starblaze said, "My parents worked in remediation, my grandparents toiled in Geo-engineering, all their lives trying to heal the wounds made by previous generations. Did they succeed or fail? Here we are, still living. This boat we sit in floats on the high water mark, unless an asteroid made of ice fell to Earth, it wont get any higher than this. If you were a pessimist you might call that failure. Even reading all the old spiritual texts you can see that when god started playing god, he knew he was in over his head."

"Set a ball rolling downhill and see if you can stop it. God." Duffy said, "A concept that's starting to come back in fashion, perhaps for the opiate-like calming effect that faith has on troubled people."

"I'm not trying to believe in god, but I'm not saying that she doesn't exist. How presumptuous would that be! We science loving people cant even proove where the universe came from. They can talk about math and tell you about a big bang they heard, but that's about as deep as saying you saw a baby come out from between a mother's legs. We're just babies. We know so little we might as well call it nothing. We left the planet a couple times back then but now we're just running to survive. Used to study the rise and fall of nations, now we only study the decline. People still argue if we should even be trying to survive or just let go and enjoy life until it ends. Really ends. If it's too late, then let's get out our bucket list and party it up. You know we engage in that mind sometimes, you cant deny it. A person can't live in a state of worry all the time. You have to let go sometimes or you'll burn out."

The skiff rose and fell thru several waves, enuf time that Duffy might have yawned and laughed and shrugged and moved on to a different subject, but within he felt a strange surge of fire like when moving the cello bow on a fat low string then switching to a higher string, buoyed upwards by successive waves of sound emotion. Duffy turned to Starblaze with a smile, "I believe we are going to make it."

The freighter loomed large now, a thousand meters long, the deck painted white and the sides below waterline painted dark red, two cargo cranes painted yellow had been converted into jumbo sails with a silver composite material that caught the wind and also worked as solar electricity collector wired to run the large electro turbine that drove the ship's propeller. In the rear of the ship was a five story steel building with pilot house atop, a floating apartment building. On the deck could be seen a small orchard of fruit trees and tall rows of food crops.

A ramp lowered from the cliff-like hulk of the Merry Gentleman and the skiff slid nicely onto it, they were soon lifted into the shade of the dry dock amidships where a dozen people stood waiting. Captain Margerite made introductions as they moved to a stair that led up onto the sunny top deck where a huge and well tended garden stretched into the distance. The apple trees had been pruned with an artists hand, the vegetable gardens loved into fruition, the leaves of the bean vines fluttered in the gulf breeze like pennants.

"During a storm we raise the greenhouse shutters from both sides, and no worries." Captain Margerite said. On the grass playground the refugee children were welcomed by the ship children and were soon playing hide and seek in the fragrant dill and fennel bushes.

Captain Margerite led them to some long benches made of split spruce logs, bark still on the round outsides with a large quarter cut out lengthwise for sitting.

"We turned around to meet you." Margerite said, "After the hurricane passed we counted ourselves fortunate to have predicted the path so accurately. When we got your call we came at speed."

"We appreciate this." Starblaze said, "It must be expensive to operate a ship this size."

"My enthusiasm is selfish, I want questions answered. Are you still having the dreams?"

Starblaze nodded yes.

*   *   *

"Hello? Jameson?" Duffy held one finger in his ear, the other hand gripped a phone pressed against his open ear, "Yes, its me. I lost my phone, an awesome story I'll tell you sometime. How are you? And my cafe?"

Duffy was silent as he listened, then laughed in the small bunk room he and Starblaze had been issued, the dull painted walls echoed loudly, "Yes, OUR cafe, I am aware of the governing structure."

Silent again, Duffy listened while outside the room's round window a seagull cried and water crashed against the hull, "No they cant permanently seize my operations during an emergency leave of absence. You filed the papers for me, with the signatures I left, yes?" Silence. "Okay you didn't file the papers. Here is a very important question for you Jameson: did you betray me, or just completely fail our friendship?"

Duffy listened to Jameson.

"Hmmm. You can fix it? I have my doubts. Tell them I am on my way back. I'll be asking the collective for a special exemption. I want you to do this now. Do it now. I mean NOW. I'll call you back. Bye. Yes, okay, bye."

Duffy looked at the phone he had borrowed from Karpay Lee and set it down on a shelf instead of throwing it, and looked out the portal at the undulating waters, breathing in and then breathing out. Always with the suffering, Duffy thot, you know what would make these breathing exercises more effective is if people stopped doing all those irritating things.

Duffy lay down on the bed to rest but his eyes would not close, the were kept open by the memories of his life in New Bear which might be at an end if his holdings were seized. What then, back to mopping floors? No, he would hit the road, head North again, join the windmill crews perhaps, the open range, it was beautiful there at least. When Duffy rose to his feet again he left the room and walked down the metal hall until he found the door back to the open deck, dusk had come and the stars were shining over the open water so brightly they reflected and it seemed like the ship was sailing thru the galaxy. A tiny fire burned up near the bow and in the dark it shone like a small sun. Duffy made his way slowly thru the gardens to the fire pit where crew and refugees told stories and shared food and drink under a warm Gulf breeze.

"Have a seat!" Starblaze called him over, Duffy sat next to her.

"You would never know there was anything wrong with the world walking into a scene like this."

Across the fire Ruth crawled playfully from lap to lap in a game of keep-off-the-ground, and when she came to David she laughed and grabbed mischievously at his head of thick black hair which came off in her hands as she fell forward, David caught her and set her safely down. Ruth stood before the fire with a black wig in hand while the man's real blond hair fell over his frightened blue eyes. The fugitive!

28

Pagnellopy awoke in the tall grass of Light Hollow curled next to the hard back shell of Xippix, surprisingly warm to snuggle a turtle, Pagnellopy thot, blinking at the suns rising. Pagnellopy untangled from the leathery green arms and stood up. It seemed like they were alone in the meadow, no cats in sight, the tall boulder was unoccupied. Xippix noticed Pagnellopy had risen and extended arms and legs to stretch, "Is this the same day, or the next day?"

Pagnellopy looked at Xippix, "I had a strange dream."

"I had a dream too." Xippix said, "There was a strange ship sailing under a strange sun."

"The square ship with a jungle on top and a big yellow sun in the sky and people with smooth skin and fuzzy heads." Pagnellopy said.

"Many shades of skin but all smooth as an underbelly, no hide, shell, bumps, and only two eyes. The language they spoke was so high pitched, almost like the mating song of the shum-shum fly." Xippix had distant eyes, "We had the same dream?"

A massive energy discharge came from the woods and a scream tore across the peaceful meadow. Pagnellopy ran after the noise while Xippix stood confused.

"Wait!"

Pagnellopy ran, hearing more horrible high pitched screams, and reaching the forest Pagnellopy smelled wood and flesh burning, the unmistakable acrid odor of burnt hair. Flashes of light betrayed the location of the shooter, Pagnellopy moved in that direction slightly more cautiously. From behind a massive trunk Pagnellopy stepped out to see the smoking body of a Coqolot on the forest floor, it's legs unmoving. Around the Coqolot many trees and shrubs were in flames and smoking, thick trunks now sliced in half, blackened and smoldering. A flash of light burst from a dense stand of shrub and a howl erupted, far off they watched a cat with fur smoking run at full speed thru the forest and disappear, chased by chaotic flashes of deadly energy. Chartles stepped into the open with a long black gun and a strange look, as if this were a normal day at school and this was simply an assignment that must be completed. Pagnellopy walked towards Chartles.

Xippix' mouth moved and formed the word "No!" but no sound came out, Xippix' vocal chords refused to attract Chartles attention to the presence of a best friend who seemed to have spontaneously chosen noble death. Xippix then noticed something new, a light surrounding Pagnellopy's head, a glow like that of the cats when they communed among themselves and the universe. A trick of the suns shining down thru forest foliage? The glow became brighter until Xippix knew there was no way Pagnellopy would fail to be seen by Chartles, in a moment it would be over when the trigger went back and a flash of energy took someone that Xippix dearly loved away. Xippix prepared to leap and scream and do anything but allow that to happen.

Chartles turned and saw Pagnellopy, but did not bring the gun to bear. Now a strange look took hold of Chartles face, the reflection of a struggle that went all the way to the very roots of being. And then Chartles was flying thru the air, hands empty and clutching at nothing, screaming in pain under the claws of a massive bird Xippix had never seen this close up and wondered if it was a species only known to the Light Forest. A rush of winged wind pushed against everything as the bird lifted Chartles up thru a hole in the canopy of the forest where a great old tree had long ago fallen and let the light of the suns shine into the darkness, and then the great bird and Chartles were gone.

29

In the large main dining hall of the Merry Gentleman they all gathered quietly and sealed the doors.

"Before you exited the train you claimed to be on our side and said you could prove it." Duffy said to the refugee, "You owe us a word."

"The word I never had a chance to say is Gaeiou."

"The dream planet." Captain Margerite said, and the room nodded.

"Interstellar Quantum Consciousness." said the blond haired fugitive, "There is no way to prove it. There may never be a way to prove it. So when I say Interstellar Quantum Consciousness it's almost the same thing as saying it's all in your mind. Your mind is wired to the cosmos, and if someone wanted to they could read yours, or you could read theirs."

"Are you a scientist?" Captain Margerite said.

"I was. Little demand for quantum physicists in our present day situation. Nobody wants to hear the math of wave particle duality anymore. You have to pass yourself off as a coder or engineer, something a bit more practical."

"If the dream is from another planet," Captain Margerite continued, "How could it be transmitted to us over cosmic distances? Even at the speed of light the vision would be ancient."

"It could be happening there just as we are experiencing it here. Particles at two different points in space time acting simultaneously but not connected by any known forces or structures. We used to call this behavior of quantum particles spooky action at a distance."

"This is not the first time I've heard this theory." Duffy said.

Starblaze Sturgeon leaned forward, "Have you murdered?"

"No."

"You answer too fast!"

"What!?"

"Is your name really David?"

"Are you asking him this because he's white?" Karpay Lee said.

"Or because he is a refugee?" Captain Margerite said.

"We saw him in the act of violence!" Duffy said, "We heard screams."

"I hope you have more evidence than words. Where is the victim?" Captain Margerite said.

The blue eyed man spoke, "You saw something you can't explain."

"There were screams." Duffy put his hands in the air.

"Another passenger witnessed the same thing." Starblaze said.

"Exactly. You all saw the same thing." the blond man smiled, "You saw a private ritual to rid myself of these haunting recurring dreams, the spirits of which I believed had tormented me to follow you. Sleep deprivation and dehydration have terrible effects on the mind. I have a different theory now. I believe we are being contacted by another sentient species in the universe, or multiverse, or somethingverse. Language fails me. Something real is happening in a very unreal way and everyone in this room is tied to it."

Captain Margerite straightened her spine, "Look around this room, a very diverse group. Totally random selection or purposeful representation of all the peoples left on earth."

"Mathematical." Karpay Lee said.

"We all feel this vision is real." the refugee continued, "but is it really off world or is it manufactured on Earth? It must be more probable to have come from Earth."

"I can imagine about a dozen sources." Starblaze said, "We could all be unwilling participants in a mind control experiment."

"Some of us may not be so innocent." Duffy looked at the blue eyed man.

"There are more on the way." Captain Margerite said, "Another ship with people like us. I am in contact with them, you may look at the logs if you wish."

"How many?" Duffy answered.

"Hundreds."

The room was silent and then Starblaze Sturgeon cleared her

throat, "So what shall we do? Keep dreaming?"

"First, let's have lunch. Objections? Good. Toast with jalapeno strawberry jam." Captain Margerite flagged the robo waiter.

"What should we call you?" Duffy asked the refugee.

"My name is Louis Garfield."

"Duffy Shoreman."

30

The cats licked wounds in the forest and their ears flicked and spun alertly, listening to every noise even the fall of a single pine needle. They had not evolved and survived on this tough world without being always awake, even while sleeping. The cat who welcomed them to Light Hollow approached Pagnellopy, "A hidden ability has been awakened. Welcome."

Pagnellopy glowed with a faint light and no words could be heard in the air.

"Thank you. I am aware of the light awakening in toad and turtle people, but I did not expect to be one of them. I feel I will now always have a reason to smile."

The cat purred.

Xippix returned from the clearing under the forest canopy where they had last seen Chartles, "I have a question. How many of those jumbo birds hunt around here, and should we be worried about that?"

Pagnellopy smiled and the cat slow blinked appreciation, "We don't have to worry about the birds, Xippix. I can talk to them now. It's a good thing."

"Yeah, I saw that. Is Chartles dead?"

"He's been returned home. When there are changes in the world some people will lash out in anger, having perceived that their way of life is threatened. There is never a way of life that we can forever own and not have to share it sometimes with the rest of the world. We live on this planet together. We must embrace the anger, hold these people close and listen, make them feel safe, or this will all happen again. You can't kill evil. The potential exists inside everyone."

Xippix's turtle head drooped, "I guess this changes everything."

31

The jalapeno strawberry jam was gone. Duffy felt the tingle of the food in his body radiating out from his stomach, with such an excellent thing to eat in the world how could there not be a real possibility for people to rally in this final hour and produce solutions to the crisis that unbalanced the environment and killed half the human population.

Duffy and Starblaze stood on the bridge with Captain Margerite and Karpay Lee studying the animated map. Gulf waters undulated below the hulls of numerous ships on a radial grid, in the center of the map an island.

"Seven ships of various size all converging. Some we are in contact with and some are keeping communication silence. Drawing a direct line from each ship, excluding those which are on course to rendezvous with us, the destination is a small rocky island 9 square kilometers in size. The island is not on the charts."

"How can something not appear on a satellite map?"

Captain Margerite nodded, "Rumors of floating structures, amalgamations of old old drilling platforms covered with materials even including soil and plants to make them appear like uninhabited islands. Potentially secret government seats, they could move to evade storms or just anchor down. They could be loaded with defensive capabilities. There could be anything or anyone in there. I am not enthusiastic. The Merry Gentleman has limited defensive drones."

"How is the forecast?"

"Good for days." Karpay Lee said, " We will arrive at island in clear sky and warm weather."

"More questions, but this destination feels like it will have answers." Captain Margerite said, "Some of the converging ships are requesting an update from the two of you."

"Us?" Duffy said.

"It seems that you and Starblaze feature in many reports about the link to the other world. Someone is promoting you. It is a mystery to me. If you want to talk to the other ships, here is the talking stick, it's ready to go."

Starblaze took the small black rod and looked at Duffy, "Lets find a quiet place and simply say what we're thinking."

"Nothing surprises me now. The fourth and fifth wall are gone. Before it's all over there won't be a roof either." Duffy said and followed Starblaze to a small room where they closed the door, "I'll go first. It will be worse if I have to listen to you and think about what I should say." he twisted the device and it glowed blue, "Today we stand on Earth. Long ago our ancestors stopped putting greenhouse gasses into the atmosphere but still the temperature rose. Leaders balked at the methane sequestration protocol because it redirected energy away from pleasurable

179

activities to focus on a project that would consume the efforts of a generation. Maintaining the permafrost. Shutting down the feedback loops. Austerity. Survival. Could we do it? Earth as a place that humans might continue living. We still have the spark! The fire inside burning, moving towards necessary deeds."

Duffy handed the talking stick to Starblaze and she spoke, "Our experience is not an illusion or an introspective dream. There is only one thing that can bring us to a triumphant conclusion and that is a universal love. When I say universal love I mean inter-stellar, inter-galactic, and inter-dimensional love. Something beyond our understanding, there are no words for it. Life is everywhere. To see the big picture you step back, but how far back can you step? Far enuf and the snake begins to eat it's own tail. Are we being guided towards a conclusion that is not our own, or are we directing ourselves towards this, unconsciously, as an interconnected group? Nothing feels inescapable to me. Anyone could leave at any moment and there would be no immediate consequence, but a greater good might loose critical mass and be abandoned. So we continue to follow our dreams. This island like a magnet draws us in, those who share the vision, we trust intuition. Yes this could be something evil. One would be arrogant to believe they knew everything. We don't know everything and so we continue looking for answers. Pleasant dreams."

Starblaze twisted the stick and the glow ceased.

"That's it." Starblaze Sturgeon said to Duffy Shoreman, "Get some good sleep tonight. Tomorrow is the day."

The sun fell below a high layer of clouds in the west and sent invigorating rays to fill the air of New World Gulf as the drummers with their long drum sticks sat in circle around a big drum placed in the garden courtyard amidships. Sweat fell like melted snowflakes on the white painted steel deck as the drummers became the rhythm. Crossing worlds, they were joined by others unseen and sang out strongly the words of a new song the elders had never taught and they had never before heard.

32

"We don't have it so bad on Gaeiou." Pagnellopy said to Xippix as they hiked the trail back to town.

"Compared to the dream of Earth?" Xippix said.

"They suffered greatly. Another spinning globe out in the darkness. Do you think we could ever figure where in the sky we should look to see their sun?"

Thru a break in the trees they could see a great swath of stars undiminished by the lights of Heart City far away.

"We still live in our homes, in the places we were born. Things are getting worse for us, but we don't suffer like the smooth skin people of Earth. On Gaeiou we are the generation that could shrug and forget about it all, climate change isn't going to affect our generation much."

"It's all relative, any generation could stop caring. Turtle people a hundred years ago loved snow, my Grandstar used to slide down hills covered in snow, riding on his back shell, feet in the air, that's how turtles did it. To hear them tell the stories they seem to think we suffer for having too much of a good thing. The differences in seasons is what made winter so exciting. Now winter is so long that nobody gets joy out of it anymore, and by the end you're lucky to not be on hibernation medication."

"Big picture." Pagnellopy said, "The balance must return. We cannot accept the extinction of life on Gaeiou."

"If we little creatures changed the climate, we can change it back."

"In our lifetime?"

"We are young. Why not."

Pagnellopy stopped on the trail, noticing a Shum-Shum fly landing on the side of a tree. Tongue shot forth, the fly was quickly down toad throat.

"Hmmm, so tasty wild caught." Pagnellopy held their hand on the bark of the tree and looked up into the green canopy of the trees, "The Long Summer is soon to end, storm season coming. What should we do, our next step?"

"We've only just planted the seeds." Xippix sat on a mossy log next to the trail, "During the quiet inside time we must keep organizing and sharing the knowledge, even if everyone in the universe received our message we have to keep educating because people forget and new people are born every day. People wake up with a story and they learn, but if there is nothing more to fill them, ignorance and hate will carve deep ruts and be difficult to heal. We have to continue educating ourselves and everyone else for as long as we are alive. It never stops, we have to keep talking or the balloon of understanding that surrounds us will collapse and we will suffocate. Cultural inertia we are fighting is strong, it still exists as hatred in my Grandstars. We can never let up or the world will go back to the ignorant ways when turtles and toads killed each other. We can never let that happen again."

"You got it." Pagnellopy said, "If I get depressed, remind me of this conversation."

The two walked along the forest trail for many hours, emerging sometimes in a rocky ravine with a mountain stream flowing down, places that seemed like they had always been there. They came to an overlook where Heart City was visible, far below on the valley floor, a spread of colorful domes amid a forest of green, and outside the city and into the foothills spread the patterns of large insect farms and arched greenhouses. Circles scattered about were little ponds and lakes where fish were farmed.

"I can see our school." Pagnellopy said.

"I always thot we would go back to school next season and all this would be over. I can hardly imagine going back there now. We are changed."

"It wont be the same. We've spent the summer swimming in a different sea. We still have so much to learn."

"We also have to teach the teachers. The world we want to inherit when the old ones die is not the world most of them have made for us. I hope they have seen the vision, I hope it resonates in them. If not we have to do it again and keep talking."

"Not it." Pagnellopy moved turtle hands in a scissors motion, "Let's bring my Grandstar some of the spiced jumble bug mix, we can pick it up in Two Lakes."

"Mm, and we can pick up another bag of fish like we gave to the cats."

"I'm hungry too."

"Down we go then." Xippix said and they strolled along the descending wooded trail.

An hour later Pagnellopy stopped and leaned against a tree, "These toad legs are tired!"

"We cant stop again or we won't make Two Lakes by market close!"

"How about a ride then?"

"Okay rabbit legs, but don't tell anyone." Xippix dropped to all fours and Pagnellopy jumped onto turtle back shell and squatted there, Xippix moved awkwardly rumbling down the trail in a reversal of evolution's desire, on all fours.

"So Pagnellopy, you have a new ability and I don't have that. Now you're riding on my back. Are we still gonna have a friendship of equals?"

Pagnellopy launched toad tongue to the back of Xippix's turtle neck and it stuck there a moment before retracting, Xippix shuddered in surprise, "Okay Xippix, how about this. Whenever you want to borrow the glow, call me and I'll come over."

"Great. Let's go fishing soon, with the birds on our side we'll be famous."

33

The Merry Gentleman ran at full speed, wakes rolling from the bow and a storm of propeller wash behind, undulating currents in the water all around spinning fish in circles. Ahead on the horizon a long dark shape appeared on the sparkling waters. Duffy was now above decks and squinted into the sunlight. He found sunglasses in a pocket of the wind breaker the captain had given him to wear, as he put the sunglasses on they beeped and a tactical display appeared, zooming in on the focal point of his eyes. The shape on the horizon was a substantial island according to the data. Duffy put the phone borrowed from Karpay Lee in his ear and called Jameson.

"Jameson! Any news?"

"Plenty. I've been posting all the updates you've told me and also re-posted the inspirational broadcasts you've sent to the other ships and now it seems you have really thousands of followers, its incredible. Most of them passed thru your cafe actually. The Far North sold out every day! I hired someone to help restock the robo cook, we were slinging tubes like Festival of Silence wild asses. A good part of these people are now somewhere out on the gulf headed to meet you and everyone else. Too many for the tribal police to stop!"

"Viral."

"Congratulations and you're welcome. I don know what you have planned but it seems like it should be a good party."

A sound came from Duffy's mouth which frightened the gulls loitering on the railing and they flew off, squawking, "This is not what I asked you to do. I asked you to appeal to the Cafe Circle to recognize special circumstances so that I can retain my business and home, I may have a warrant with tribal police, and you have laid all my cards on the table. What's in it for you? Did you sell these people tickets to a vacation? Did you double the prices and pocket tips from my cafe? None of this makes sense, unless I have been betrayed."

"These people share the vision Duffy, that's all. Something is happening that I have never seen before. Many of them are young, some of them old, all ages, all kinds of people. Ridiculously optimistic if you ask me. This cannot turn out as good as they hope it will. I'm just a jaded middle age man I guess, perhaps if I didn't sleep so soundly every night I would have the dream too. I'm a little jealous. Perhaps tonight I will set an alarm and wake up during dream sleep. I support you, Duffy, and your crew. People in the triple C have the vision too."

"The Circle?"

"Yeah! You've got it Duffy, you're good! They support you. No worries. If you survive this revolution or whatever is brewing out there you'll be welcomed back with honors I believe. They might even let you keep that crappy cafe."

Revolution? Duffy's head throbbed with anxiety and suspicion. Too much. He let his shoulders drop and looked out on the island growing larger in his vision. Duffy allowed his regular breathing to return and decided to trust in the possibility that Jameson actually was his friend.

"I'm contemplating the possibility that you may be telling the truth."

"That's great Duffy. Real progress."

* * *

Everyone was on the deck of the Merry Gentleman looking to the island, some dressed for action and survival, some dressed in formal attire, some like Starblaze Sturgeon dressed in flashy but practical night club outfits with spectacular hairdos which sparkled in the sun. There were many different concepts about what fashion one should wear when confronting the unknown. A great exchange of information had been going non-stop since the previous night and grew exponentially as they came into contact with other ships who's passengers came aboard and in speaking thru conference rooms to those further away, a consensus was arrived at, and now Captain Margerite announced it on the news feed:

"I address the vision circle as a diverse group representing many racial, cultural, regional, and linguistic groups which remain on

Earth. We who are assembled here now are about to confront the power of the old world, still active and entrenched, assembled inside this secret island fortress. Being successful in this confrontation will allow us to take the next step to make future life on Earth possible. This is the consensus of the visions."

A great cheer rang out across the ship and thru all the ships on the gulf.

"Regarding the subject of planet Gaeiou, consensus was not achieved. Some believe the planet actually exists, some believe it does not, some thot it was metaphorical mind control but maybe a good kind because it was inspiring a good thing. No one could remember the last time they felt so confident, inspired, and alive in the face of potential doom. So it has been decided. To the island!" Another cheer went up, the bridge crew of the Merry Gentleman roared and their voices were carried thru the captain's mic and into the news feed.

"Let's do this." someone shouted and those on deck cheered again, howling and holding their fists in the air.

An audible alarm went off and the crew disappeared below decks. The blue eyed man who's name was revealed to be Louis Garfield pointed in the direction of the island and shouted. In the sky between the ship and the island a dozen black spots moved. Duffy tried to think of happy things, a flock of geese? No, their movement was too steady for birds.

"Drones." Duffy said, "How could they get away with firing on us, we are citizens! Most of us."

"Accidents happen." Starblaze clamped her jaw, "Maybe hold your ID up to the sky? Come on Duffy!" Starblaze ran to the refugees on deck, "Everybody below decks!" she picked up Ruth and ran for the stairs, the crowd on deck scattered.

"We did not come here to hide!" one of the refugees shouted, a man with short black curled hair and black skin, he stood between the anxious refugees and the approaching drones, "Join together! Put your fist in the air, your left fist and left arm which is closest to your heart, those fingers wrapped together is us together right now. Give your heart to the vision, let them see you and give the drone pilots love!"

The drones were close now, those still on deck could see the bomb pods under the wings. Two of the drones cut away sharply and rose above the others, slowing down they fell to the rear of the delta, dozens of white smoke trails sped from the two drones towards the formation. Explosions rocked the sky as missiles connected with drones. Those still on deck dove for cover as debris rained down and made loud clanging noises as it bounced off the steel ship.

The two drones that remained turned away from the ship, one dipped it's wings side to side several times, then both drones dove straight down and crashed into the Gulf waters.

34

The artificial island filled the long windows of the bridge on the Merry Gentleman, a dark gray stretch of rock and scattered forests with blue sky above and green ocean below.

"Captain." Karpay Lee said while pointing at a zoom of the island. Captain Margerite examined the large image, a dozen oval balloons floating several kilometers high and tethered to the island with black lines. Zooming further in the line was revealed to be a hose with multiple spigots spaced along its length, each one spraying a vapor which emerged as a mist but soon became the same temperature as the atmosphere and disappeared.

"Geo-engineering." the science officer said, "Question is, what is the composition of that mist?"

"Do we have a beach?" Captain Margerite said.

"There is a bay, deep enuf we can make landing."

"We don't have time to anchor and shuttle everyone ashore on skiffs. Run the Gentleman aground on the beach and prepare to debark with haste using all available methods. Those who can repel on ropes go first. Fire the zip line harpoon before anyone goes ashore. Those unable to descend by rope will go in the zip line basket or on the skiff. Set security on automatic and prepare to abandon ship."

The helm control officer turned from the controls a moment, and opened her mouth, a meeting of the collective could be called in this moment to vote on recalling the captains election. Instead of this option, the helm control officer studied the face of the one who ordered this drastic course, and so would later recall the look on that face in retelling the story much later in life to a future generation. The helm control officer closed her mouth and turned back to the controls, setting course to ground the ship on the mystery island.

"Best speed. Stay alive." Captain Margerite said, "I have my ears on, I'll be at the bow."

Karpay Lee kept his eyes on the screens as the Captain left the bridge tho he was not thinking about anything on the screens.

Ruth had climbed the tallest tree on deck, a white pine that towered as tho it would one day offer itself up as mast of the ship, and there from it's crown she looked to the horizon. The island was close now, she could see gulls flying over the beach hunting fish and washed up crustaceans.

A chickadee landed on a branch and looked at Ruth with it's head cocked.

"Hello!" Ruth said, "Do you live here?"

The bird jumped and spun around to land on the branch again, getting a different perspective on Ruth.

"Do you ever leave the ship? Or does the Captain feed you?"

The chickadee chirped, flew to a branch farther away, then sang it's full song.

"I wouldn't mind living on this ship. It's a nice place. I like everyone I've met here."

The chickadee blinked.

Ruth looked at the horizon again.

"We're going to that island. Do you think you might fly around there? The island has nice trees."

The chickadee flew away. From her perch Ruth could see other ships converging on the island, some very close, headed to the same beach the Merry gentleman was headed for. The ship sailed into the island's defense perimeter and insect sized information drones swarmed around them, buzzed thru the air, moving in zig-zag scanning patterns. The song birds all became quiet. The ship's defensive mini drones emerged, looking like dragon flies, which caught the islands info drones and bit them in half, and a gentle metal rain fell on the deck.

Ruth looked below, people were gathering at the bow, preparing methods for lowering themselves to the beach and strapping backpacks to each other. Ruth saw her mother with the other refugees, preparing to make landfall on the island. The ship felt safe, Ruth thot. But if everyone left, she would be alone here, and alone was never safe.

Ruth thot about how she must go down and down and down and put her feet on the ship and down again to the shore and walk thru the salty water to climb thru the forests of the island and face what was there, just like Pagnellopy on the planet Gaeiou. It was scary but if they did it together it might be okay. Ruth's skin tingled as she began to climb down the pine tree.

Louis moved among the people gathered at the bow of the Merry Gentleman, "No weapons, please. No lengths of metal the scanner could mistake for weapons. No flammable liquids, the scans can detect that. Food, water, phones, lights are okay. If you insist on bringing weapons, you must be the last ones to leave the ship. These are the protocols."

"We have the fire of our spirits." Starblaze said.

Duffy wondered if it was a line from a play, or if she was writing one now in her mind, "Do you believe that?"

"We have already survived the fire in the sky. Death from above will not take us today. We are a movement that runs thru everything like the mycelium under mushrooms, and this is our day after the rain, it is our time to flower."

Duffy folded his arms looking up at the looming island, "I don't like this."

"Every person on this planet is afraid, Duffy."

The ship entered the bay and evergreen tree covered outcrops rushed by as the harbor emerged before them. The ship charged the beach and a deep multi voiced bellowing horn shook the rib cage of every person on board, with no less than three full blasts of pressurized air thru that instrument a sound like a chorus of 10,000 buffaloes, whales, elephants, wolves, and bears. The ship's bow rose up as they hit the beach and the Merry Gentleman lurched to a hard stop throwing everyone into a dog pile at the bow. A large wave pushed by the ship crashed over the beach of the mysterious island and then there was silence. Duffy found himself near the top of the dog pile, in the embrace of Louis, legs bent, balancing as the ship came to rest. Louis smiled as Duffy stood back up and let go of everything.

35

The island was heavily overgrown with tangle vines and a multitude of insects sang a merry symphony with legs and wings rubbing together. The heat of summer had returned with the passing of the hurricane from the Gulf and the business of hunting and eating was on minds of all sizes. While the two leggeds crawled out of their giant steel floating shell, thru the salty sand and into the luscious vines, one thousand insects on the island mated and shared DNA, one hundred thousand insect children were conceived at the landing of the visionary mammals on the island that had no name but was their home. The insects continued eating and mating, hyper aware of the present moment, the future was a silent plan.

The first group on shore found a lack of trails so they took a small animal path into the jungle, Ruth had discovered it. The crew crawled on hands and knees up the hill, hoping that the path might open up at a higher elevation. It was a long time crawling, Ruth, Duffy, Starblaze, Louis, and Mary, Ruth's mother. The animal trail split into three, they chose to crawl up the path that seemed to have the most light at the end. Only Ruth was not complaining, hoping on all fours like a bunny.

"Be a rabbit." she said to Duffy.

"I am suffering." Duffy said.

Starblaze Sturgeon spoke, "Good for me I accepted the role as Cockroach #4 in a performance many years ago. I rehearsed and performed this very type of crawling sixty-two times."

"Difficult on the back." Duffy said.

The animal path emerged at a plateau and they unfolded themselves vertically to a woodland scene which included a small pond. As they circled the pond all the turtles that had been sunning themselves on logs dove into the water, and as they walked in the tall grass toads sprang away from their feet. On the far side of the pond they came upon a small wooden dock shrouded by cat tail plants with two birch bark canoes pulled up on shore. A human trail led up and away from the pond following a small creek. Up and up they climbed.

"I think someone is coming." Duffy said, "Let's hide in these bushes!"

They crawled into the bracken and remained silent. A minute went by. Duffy shifted a little and Starblaze shot him a freezing look. Duffy wondered if he was wrong, it was really only a strong feeling, or intuition, he hadn't actually heard or seen anything. He was about to speak and tell them he was mistaken when crashing footsteps came down the rocky trail. They watched from the bushes as several people dressed in forest camouflage and strapped with fighting gear hustled by. The visionaries remained completely silent and unmoving, but as the last warrior went by her head turned and Duffy looked directly into her eyes. All four of their eyes widened, but the warrior said nothing and continued down the trail. After a very long ten seconds Duffy whispered to Starblaze, "I made eye contact with the last person."

"Not every ally can reveal themselves, but for those in a position of power, doing nothing can be doing a lot. We have been blessed."

Louis touched Duffy's shoulder, "Keep up the good work Duffy, we need what you've got."

"We could have jumped them and taken their weapons." Mary said flexing her fingers into fists, "How can we fight them without weapons?"

"We would already be dead if we had weapons. Possessing a weapon makes you a target."

"It also makes us defenseless."

"Not true." Starblaze said, "We just defeated a squad of warriors without engaging them. Our weapon is the vision that has already been spread across the planet. We are behind their lines and we are in their minds. We have friends here. Our vision has been here for days. Their gun is our gun."

"They will hold their fire." Louis said.

"Most of them." Duffy said, "I've been running the numbers in my head. I'm a businessman, it's my job. The exponential effect in this movement has reached critical mass. Only a small percentage of warriors will now actually follow contrary orders in the face of so many comrades refusing. If you see a gun pointed at you, then you have met that small percentage."

"If this occurs, fall to the ground and wait for our allies to respond." Louis said.

"Let's go!" Ruth clambered out of the bracken and pushed aside the tangle vine, followed by the rest.

The trail became winding as they climbed, switching back and forth they reached a bald bluff and carefully moved out onto the barren rock face. Now exposed to the sky they glanced upwards, wondering. Over the edge of the bluff a carpet of green trees spread out all the way to the blue waters of the harbor, beyond the wild green waves of the Gulf. In the bay the reassuring bulk of the Merry Gentleman sat nosed into the beach where they had left it. Other ships now also lined the beach and even still approached the island, pushing into the bay.

"We surprised them, they were not prepared for such a landing." Louis said.

"Drone reinforcements could be hours away."

"We must achieve our goal before they arrive."

"This way!" Ruth said and ran up the rim trail followed by her mother.

"Wait, look at that boat on the outer edge, it's tribal police!" Duffy said.

"That boat belongs to me." a familiar voice from behind said. They all turned to see a figure step from the trail they had just emerged from and level a weapon at them: the Inspector from the hurricane battered train!

36

"I see the fugitive is here with you." the Inspector eyed Louis, "If you are innocent of all else you are definitely wanted for involvement in a violent incident on my train. Twelve innocent passengers forcibly disabled as you fled the scene. It is illegal to ignore people in distress. Twelve counts of abandonment. Have you ever been disabled by one of these?" she pointed the energy weapon directly at Louis, "An unpleasant experience at best."

"My apologies Inspector." Louis said, "It sounds strange to me as the words form in my mouth, but here it is: I was motivated by the dream of a better world and meant no harm to anyone."

"I have a job to do, but I did not know how I would respond to this meeting until now. That is a first for me. I've been searching many days, last night I had a vision while I slept." the inspector lowered her gun, "As I look at these familiar faces before me, there is nothing else that explains this situation. Whatever matters of petty justice need to be satisfied can wait until the greater cause is served. Now in this moment, this very day, everything is going to change."

"Join us!" Starblaze said, "We follow the child. She knows."

Ruth waved and smiled to the inspector from the trail head up the bluff, the inspector smiled back and holstered her weapon.

"The weapon." Starblaze said, "You must leave it, or we will be targeted by automatic systems."

The inspector looked from person to person, then nodded and removed the holster from her hip, stashing it in the bracken.

The moment was shattered by a long bellow from the Merry Gentleman's air horns, short blasts which repeated without cease.

"There!" Starblaze pointed at the sky where a white vapor trail stretched from the horizon to a point of fire above them.

"Take cover!" the Inspector screamed and dashed to the trail, grabbing Ruth she ducked behind a large boulder, followed by everyone else. The detonation in the harbor sent a flash of white light illuminating the woods in a way the trees had never seen, in the next second a sonic blast rippled thru their bodies and the boulder they sheltered behind moved. A column of fire and smoke rolled into the sky followed by a hot rain that fell on them as they huddled. Slowly each stood and returned to the bluff, the wreck of the Merry Gentleman was scattered on shore but in the bay there was nothing but water, the other boats previously anchored in the bay were now lodged in trees onshore, crushed and broken.

"This was in my dream." Ruth said, and there were tears on her face, "This way! Let's go!" she led them up the trail.

The group hustled across a wooden bridge and again switch backed to the top of another ridge and followed that up to a grand plateau that felt like the top, the smooth rock rolled away as they ran like it were a miniature earth and they were giants chasing the sun, not content to watch it rise but going to get it.

As they peaked the plateau a dark line appeared, a rectangle that was revealed to be a human made structure as they closed on it, a foreboding windowless concrete monolith atop the mountain. The structure rose fifty meters high, they approached it and then were standing in it's shadow. There was only solid rock under foot, the structure rose out of the stone like it had always been part of it, seamless, immovable, taller than the trees. The group slowed to a stop before the thing and only Ruth continued up to touch the dark gray face, "Let us in!" looking up at where the top of it ended and the sky began. There was no answer, only the wind pushing on the unmovable thing.

"If we split up and circle around we can find what we're looking for faster." Duffy said.

"No. Stay together." Ruth said.

"I don't like loitering out in the open like this. Let's use our legs." Louis said.

"This way!" Ruth trotted with the towering wall on her left and the open plateau on her right. They jogged behind her, moving along the wall of the monolith looking for something they did not know. The featureless West facing wall did not change and the similar stone underfoot went by anonymously so that it was difficult to say how much time had passed. Then a line of trees appeared on the horizon and they arrived at a corner where the wall made a sharp left turn, the South face, which ran into the distance to a seemingly infinite point.

"At least we made it to the sunny side of the street."

They continued jogging along the south face, looking from the wall to the sky and wondering if soon death from above would be there to meet them. There was nowhere to hide.

"What's that?" Starblaze pointed ahead, and when Duffy looked he was relieved to see she was pointing at the wall and not to the sky. A small black spot perhaps five meters high. No one said anything more until they stood in a half circle underneath it.

"A window." Louis said.

"It looks like a hole." Duffy said.

"If it's a window, who left it open?" the Inspector said.

"Anyone have experience with building human towers?" Starblaze said and everyone shook their head no.

"Then it's the Lift for me. Duffy, you've spent years laboring, gardening, hiking, playing cello, singing, lifting loaded robo cook tubes, I am confident this has prepared you to be a human springboard. I've seen you lift heavy things, we have an affinity, and I trust you. Here's what you'll do: stand before the wall facing out with arms and legs cocked, hands up and cupped to accept my feet when I jump up on them. You don't have trouble with leg cramps?"

"No."

"Okay then. I will run towards you and leap, my feet will meet your hands and you will grab them and at that moment you will spring up and thrust with legs and at the limit of our legs extensions you push with your arms and I will extend my legs, my forward momentum will carry me up and into the window. You must put everything you've got into it. Everything."

"This is a very technical maneuver I have never tried before nor even seen performed." Duffy said, looking up at the hole in the wall.

"Look at me." Starblaze put her palms on his temples and moved into his eyes, "Wake up!"

"Okay. Summon the fire. A slap on both cheeks will do it." Duffy tucked his tongue up onto the roof of his mouth and stood still for Starblaze, she backhanded his right cheek, then open palm slap to his left cheek. Duffy felt the burning.

"Are you with me now? Can you feel the anger? Let the fire spread and let's fly."

Duffy stretched and shook out his limbs, bent upside down and rolled back up, windmilled his arms and jogged in place, "Let's do this!"

Starblaze stepped back thirty meters and motioned for him to move a finger width to the right, and then gave thumbs up. Ruth, Mary, Louis, and the Inspector sat silent, faces turned away as instructed by Duffy to help his concentration. Duffy squatted on the ground and found good footing. Starblaze and Duffy synchronized their breathing, inhaled and exhaled three times and then Starblaze leaned into the run. Duffy visualized the window above, visualized Starblaze flying up on his hands and thru the window. She jumped and as Duffy felt the wind of her feet coming down on his palms he gripped her feet and sprang and pushed and lived the entire life of a dandelion flower in less than one second, germinating and sprouting from the earth pushing ever upwards flowering opening smiling into the sun with every last cell of energy to flower bright and bursting yellow a fist of sunshine, sending into the sky the seeds of one hundred children's lives and letting them go to fly on the wind where they sailed ever upwards up and up and up. In this passionate celebration of life the dandelion Duffy saved nothing for himself and collapsed to the ground.

Starblaze hung from the rim of the opening by the tips of her fingers. She heaved up and got an elbow on the ledge, then a pair of black arms reached out and grabbed under her brown arms and Starblaze was pulled inside.

37

Pagnellopy met her Grandstar in the old garden where a group of very young toads and turtles from the neighborhood were learning about the various blooms and insects that one could see during this season. Grandstar plucked leaves, flowers, and insects from the plants and shared them with the children who marveled and recoiled at the vibrant freshness of the wild growing foods.

"Children, this is Pagnellopy, my little planet."

The children said hello in a rough chorus and Pagnellopy felt the warmth of their hearts, all the harsh toil of previous months fell away as toad sat with them. The children were sampling some of the spicy Khurillagos bush, whose zesty leaves could be put on a flesh wound to prevent infection and encourage rapid healing.

"I had a strange dream about you two nights ago." Grandstar said, "Are you feeling well?"

"I feel overwhelmed, like during Long Summer when just before Long Autumn when the sky is dark with shum-shum flies and your arms grow tired from swinging the cone net, and you send your tongue out into the sky and it comes back full of flies and your belly is already full and you are happy and tired and thinking about who you should gift all the food to and you feel invincible but really you know it's not quite true but it's fun to pretend for just awhile. Because maybe we really are immortal in some way! That's how I feel."

Grandstar smiled at Pagnellopy and turned to look at the children, "If the universe is infinite then we will continue being part of it forever. If we care for Gaeiou and keep the planet alive then we will live on in our children and our children's children. The cycle of life continues, getting a little better each time. Someday our roots will even climb off this world to explore others. Already we have shared our light."

A small turtle crawled away from the group and climbed onto Pagnellopy's folded toad legs and Pagnellopy held the child and rubbed the back of the turtle's neck which they always enjoyed.

"Your First Star needs your help in the council. Some of the old ones are bloating up again, making smug burps about bringing back the good old days."

"They cant all be brave and wise like you, Grandstar."

"One should never stop learning. The moment you decide that at last you know everything, at that moment you have returned to knowing nothing."

Another turtle crawled into Pagnellopy's lap, "Two at once!" the hard back children wrestled for favorable position, "I will go see my First Star and try to help. Between these unending labors I will take what moments I have to breathe and enjoy what surrounds me as tho there were no possible doom."

"If we don't smile when life tickles us then we may loose the ability completely." Grandstar reached out and removed a young toad that had jumped onto Pagnellopy's head.

"I may be struggling a long time," Pagnellopy put the young turtles down and they crawled back to the others, "I may have to struggle the rest of my life. It's not what I dreamed for myself at the start of this school year. So it is, this is the path I have chosen. In the middle of struggle I will also be happy. I will be happy just like these children. That is also a choice."

"I support you in every way, Pagnellopy. Come visit again soon."

38

Duffy awoke with his back against the monolith, which was not so monolithic now that it's face had been broken by the singularity of the opening thru which Starblaze had passed.

"What a strange place to take a nap. What time is it?" Duffy said.

"People!" Mary said, pointing east down the wall. A group of walkers approached and Duffy anxiously watched them with his augmented sunglasses. Soon he could see it was Captain Margerite, Karpay Lee, and the rest of the ship's bridge crew.

"Where is Starblaze?" Captain Margerite said.

"Inside." Ruth said, "She flew!"

The captain looked up but the face of the monolith was now smooth and barren. Duffy remained sitting, reclined against the wall, "It's been awhile since she went in. You've come from the other direction, no doors or windows that way?"

"Nothing."

"Did everyone escape the Merry Gentleman?"

Captain Margerite looked to the sky, "No. The ship's horn was not part of the automatic systems." she faced the wall, "We are considering launching a grapple to the roof, what do you think?"

"You have a grapple?" Duffy stood up.

Karpay Lee and Denise the cargo specialist and second navigator took the tool out from a pack and braced it's steel against the ground, following a couple checks and a warning they fired the mechanism and a steel bolt shot up to the roof trailed by a fine cable. A puff of smoke from the bolt and the four hooks deployed as it flew over the top of the structure. A wild noise of plasma discharge and hot sparks showered from the roof, the cable dropped in great coiling loops to the ground as they ducked for cover against the wall.

"Cross that off the list." Captain Margerite said while Denise quietly coiled the cable back into the bag. As a group they discussed what might be done next. After a few minutes a voice called out and they broke circle to see an open doorway at ground level not far down the wall, Starblaze Sturgeon stood outside of it.

"Oh good." Captain Margerite lead the way and soon they were inside a long dark passage, Starblaze keyed the code to close the exterior door.

"We have to close it or an alarm will activate." Starblaze said, "Yes, they know we are on the island but they don't think we can get inside."

"Now we are trapped." Duffy said.

"There are always choices." Starblaze led them down the hall, gray and featureless like the outside. They wound thru corridors and portals, carefully watching at each intersection. The control panels for the doors were opened and tiny pulled out and tampered with. They came to a door where a man wearing a security uniform stood, Duffy thot he recognized those arms, the ones that helped Starblaze get inside.

"Thru here you will become known and you must run." the guard said, "Starblaze knows the way. Lightspeed you." he pulled the door open and Starblaze shot forward.

39

Into a wide open chamber they ran, skylights illuminating the long hall. Starblaze, Duffy, Captain Margerite, Karpay Lee, Mary, Ruth, Louis, the Inspector, and the bridge crew moved swiftly in silence towards the unknown. Looking up thru the massive windows Starblaze saw in the sky a strange massive bird, bigger than any of Earth, a bird she had seen on Gaeiou. Starblaze shook off the hallucination and continued running down the hall towards a large door looming at the end.

Duffy felt a presence next to him and from the corner of his eye saw a swatch of yellow and orange tabby fur, surprised he stumbled but didn't fall thanks to Karpay Lee's steady hand on his shoulder. Duffy continued running even with the great cat of Gaeiou visibly running beside him.

"Are we dreaming?" Duffy said.

"Keep running!" Starblaze shouted, "Don't be afraid!"

Another cat appeared next to the orange tabby, a calico now, and then a black short hair with a long legged turtle riding on back, desperately gripping the fur of the cat's scruff. The cats pulled ahead of the humans with great strides and pounced thru the doors just as they were pulled open by small creatures which seemed camouflaged against the colors of the wall, but as they ran thru the doors it was clear the figures were bipedal toads. Now thru a short tunnel and out into a well lit room that was a vertical cylinder whose entire roof was a skylight. Encircling the chamber were a dozen dais with flags draped over the fronts, each with a person seated behind and several more people standing to the rear. Duffy and Starblaze stopped as the wild contents of he hallway filled the room: humans, cats, toads, turtles. Everything stopped and everyone looked at each other, everyone except Starblaze who continued walking forward until standing directly before the tallest dais of the circular council.

"Your crimes against Life on Earth are known. You may no longer profit from the destruction. You are relieved!" Starblaze demanded, "Stand and step down!"

Her voice echoed in the silent chamber and a brown skinned man with short black hair wearing an immaculate black business suit slowly rose from sitting position to stand behind the dais which bore the flag of the United Tribes, "You are very brave to come here. However, this is not an election year and I warn you that some on this council will not agree to step down, they will fight to the death to hold this power. I am not among them. I share the vision and I offer this seat of power, not to a single nation or leader, but to the citizens of a united Earth."

A lighter skinned man standing behind the president lunged forward and grappled the speaker, they fell forward on the dais as a complete melee erupted. The orange tabby sprang to the dais and removed the attacker who screamed in terror tho the cat only carried him gently, as tho moving a kitten, but the man had little scruff to be carried by.

A man standing at the dais of the Re-United States of America stood and shouted, "Guards! Guards!"

"We share the vision!" the guards near the door shouted back, and one of the warriors stepped forward, "This circle has failed the world, the blood of four billion dead stains you. Remove yourself!"

The President of the ReUnited States of America pulled a gun from his coat and aimed at the warrior, Starblaze Sturgeon shot her fist forward at the man and when her arm reached full extension her fingers opened outwards in such a violent gesture that the gunman flinched and his shot went wild. Someone from the United States of Canada dais dashed out and tackled the gunman to the ground, another shot went off and this time straight up, cracking the massive skylight. The room erupted in violence. The air surrounding the cats of Gaeiou began to glow as the brawl reached a wild fire state. Tables and chairs flew in the air, toads kicked senators with powerful legs and sprang up to land on the backs of diplomats and lobbyists. Turtles chomped on wooden chairs that were swung at them and splinters flew. The turtle riding the black cat launched forward and slid across stone floors knocking down seven entire world government delegations.

Gunfire erupted at random from the galleries, Louis, Captain Margerite, and Karpay Lee dashed to the dais of the ReUnited States of America and grappled several gunman to the floor.

Everyone had their hands on someone. Duffy managed to grab a knife wielding combatant from behind and pinned their arms in a bear hug. Was this what they had planned, or was this the plan gone awry? As Duffy contemplated the scene from the wrestler stalemate he was in, fragments of synthetic glass rained on the chamber as a swarm of jumbo birds dove thru the damaged skylight and shattered it into five billion crystal souls suitable for jewelry settings. The heads of the birds glowing gold their talons wrapped into fists they crushed those who had hunkered down firing guns, guided to their targets by the cats offering their symbiotic knowledge.

In the chaos Duffy lost his grip and the defender of the old world dashed away. As the battle raged those who shared the vision got to know each other by a look in the others eye and so they smiled even while bleeding in the mess. Some of the council began to surrender, or lay face down on the floor with large cat paws holding them down. Starblaze Sturgeon took the speaking stick from the dais at the center of the room and attached it to the news feed speaking stick from the Merry Gentleman. She spoke to the entire island complex and to the global news feed, "The old world is dead! Long live the new world. Raise your voice, everyone alive."

And then there was only the sound of agony from the dying and wounded, corrupt leaders and weary freedom fighters alike, and the sound of large cats licking their wounds.

"There's one more, somewhere there's one more. Be careful!" Duffy said and moved to where young Ruth stood watching the scene, "Ruth-" The blade struck him in the back and he collapsed as allies ran to defend him, and again screams filled the chamber.

"Ah life." Duffy whispered as he lay bleeding.

40

Pagnellopy sat in a recliner at Grandstar's garden pavilion, drinking an elixir and wincing in pain, a healing skin wrap applied to arm and torso, "I hope I never go thru something like that again."

Grandstar stood at a table next to Pagnellopy, mixing a salve for toad wounds in a small clay jar, "The heightened quantum connection between Earth and Gaeiou has returned to its usual balance, it seems. You were a mysterious key to it's collective activation. As I discuss it with Professor Klauwz, this is my understanding. He is much better at math and physics than I."

"I feel it's true. The balance may be returning, but I have changed."

Pagnellopy looked out across the valley and could see smoke from the burnt building where the circle of denial elders had made their stand. Pagnellopy survived the fight slightly wounded. Xippix was hospitalized in stable condition with painful wounds, surrounded by family. Others less fortunate lay unmoving on the ritual flat rocks, ready to be taken across the great water.

"The circle has been broken." Grandstar said, "We must be sure that all circles of people become inter-connected and form the fabric of life on Gaeiou, a weave that cannot be torn." Grandstar watched the smoke on the horizon of purple sky with Pagnellopy.

"I can only rest a short time, Grandstar. There is even more work to do."

"I offer you my garden, always."

41

Duffy lay asleep in a field of wild oats and milkweed, long towers of blue bell flowers rose up around him and somewhere high in a tree invisible birds spoke to each other in song. The sun was soon to appear, now there was only a long red line on the horizon that faded into deep blue and then into night overhead where the brilliant light of the sun reflected off Venus, and less bright but still friendly Mars and Saturn and Jupiter and a galaxy that was so much farther away but shone as bright as those single spherical mirrors of the solar system that Duffy lay in.

"Look at his eyes move, he's dreaming."

Duffy climbed invisible stairs that led to open sky above a city, the danger of falling always in mind if he stopped believing that this was possible. Higher he climbed, confidently taking giant leaps and skipping invisible steps to reach a place high above where he could see the actions of all the people in town. They moved below like ants, unaware of his existence. Someone called up to him from the ground, "Hey! You can't do that."

Duffy laughed, knowing the person was wrong, because here he was, running across the invisible staircase in the sky, leaping from one step to another to end up at a destination standing in front of the specialty popcorn vendor at the street fair. Scents of caramel, white cheddar, and salted butter rising from the crackling poppers on hot winds.

"I'll take one Trinity Bag, thank you." the booth tender smiled while grabbing a scoop, "This is a good planet."

Someone behind Duffy jostled him roughly and he turned, it was a tall person who spoke with the voice of Starblaze Sturgeon, "Duffy! It's time to go!"

Duffy opened his eyes to the morning sun shining hard on the meadow, Starblaze and others stood around him, some smiling.

"This is a good planet." Duffy said and reached to be helped up, wincing in pain as the bandaged wounds cried out. All around the meadow stood the survivors, "What happened Starblaze?"

"While you napped, we joined talking circles according to affinity and affiliations, then after discussion each circle sent a representative to the council circle, and so they spoke and wrote a new working constitution based on the consensus here."

"All that."

"Simple and profound." Starblaze pulled a scroll from her vest, "Here is your copy."

Duffy took the scroll.

"I slept thru it." Duffy stared at the paper in his hand and Starblaze laughed, "It's the painkillers. The best thing to heal your wound is rest. You did the right thing. Don't worry, you can always propose an amendment."

"We did it."

"The science officer from the Merry Gentleman has exposed the

Geo engineering they were doing with this island." Starblaze said, "The balloons we saw high up, there are hundreds of those all over and they spew out greenhouse gas. They were keeping the greenhouse effect going because it made Northern land extremely valuable. The Russians are doing the same thing."

"We interviewed old government survivors." the Inspector said, "States in the south are using these balloons to attempt reversing global heating, spraying sulfate to cool the atmosphere. The North has been battling the South with drones, destroying their balloons to keep the temperature up."

"Madness." Duffy felt lightheaded, "The years I spent in solar radiation management, trying to do the right thing. I gave half my life. Unbelievable. It's too much."

Duffy wobbled, Starblaze stepped up to avoid a fall, "Sorry old boy, we should have given you a tea first. It's been a long week."

"We have more work to do." the Inspector said, "Global Circle."

"The refugees?" Duffy looked around, "What status have they been given?"

"We are all citizens of Earth now. The singular has fallen to the plural. Look around. Ruth was elected speaker for the circle of Southern refugees, truly the youth have risen." Duffy slumped and Starblaze held him and touched his chest with gentle care, "Easy, we got this!"

"I must have lost some blood."

"Let's get you a power bite."

"And the indigenous?"

"Respected."

"Reparations?"

"The full accounting comes soon following Global Circle. The moral math is somewhat complex, but there's plenty to go around. Don't vex yourself." Starblaze led Duffy to a nearby rock and he sat upon it, "We all need to ask the spirits for help. There is a lifetime of small actions needed to heal this world. The first for you is to survive, so breathe. In and out."

"I can do that." tears rolled out of Duffy's eyes, "I have so many questions."

Duffy looked around the council circle, all the people's of the world seemed to be represented, if one could judge by appearances: gender presentations and non-gender presentations, modern social styles, cultural heritage, genetic diversity. In a world where no two people were alike, this circle felt like a spectrum that could be home to anyone.

Duffy looked down the arc of faces and laughed to see Louis in his place as one of the representatives of the Southern refugees. Not so many days ago Duffy believed the man was some kind of villain. A refugee from the South, pale skinned and not to be trusted after 600 years of every promise broken. The white man was given no love anymore, unless they had significant resources to contribute. Some prejudices arise as survival mechanisms.

Louis might still be a murderer, Duffy thot, maybe after another 600 years memory of the genocide might feel distant enuf. By then, who will they be, those descendants of the European invaders? Will they be people living in the present moment, wanting to be happy? Contemplating innocence and guilt. Nobody survived to the present day by being incompetent at murder. If you could kill an opponent and survive to pass your genes on then your children were blessed to potentially do the same. All of us killers in the old world. Eyes in the front of our head to zero in on our prey. Amazing that the concept of peace ever came into existence, but it's not, it's the evolution of evolution. Compassion for the stranger. Here at the cliff of social evolution, ready to fall or fly, we can no longer stand here contemplating the view waiting for someone to come along and push us.

"We have pushed ourselves." Duffy's eyes came back into focus and he looked to Starblaze, "Together, we take to the skies."

42

Duffy lay underneath the robo cook on a padded roller back with a scanner helmet and electric wrenches in hand, fixing a leak in the flush drain.

"Hey!"

Duffy rolled out with hands covered in black goo, he peeled off the gloves and threw them on the floor, "How can I help you?"

The person leaning over the counter wore a red hard hat with long blonde hair falling down over the counter, eyes covered by the dark sunglasses that all windmill workers wore as tho glued to their faces, "The server is busted." she stuck a thumb towards the immobile server bot, "I just want a double shot cappuccino is all."

"Alright, give me a minute."

The maintenance crews had done a minimal job on the Far north Cafe in Duffy's absence. He noted twelve different problems in the first three seconds after entering the front doors for the first time since leaving. It seemed like a very long time ago. He adjusted the flow spout on the hot drink mixer and poured a cappuccino for the worker.

"On the house. Hey, tell the crew that Duffy is back and the Far North will be fully functional later this week."

She smiled and raised the mug in salute, then headed out the door. Well, Duffy thot, at least it had been maintained to minimal standards, a robo cook that develops a glitch can create an impressive mess and cause physical harm to customers. None of that happened in his absence.

Before Duffy could return to the bowels of the robo cook the front doors opened again an Jameson strode in.

"My man, Duffy! Welcome back."

"You put a lien on my cafe while I was away on holiday."

"Only so I could hold it for you!"

"You truly believed I was returning? I often did not think I would be."

"I heard about the hurricane, and I wondered. You might say I had faith. I hear you are on the regional council now."

"It's true. Meetings three times a week right out in the garden square."

"Dang. Must be good for business."

"It is, I'm not complaining. So far, the reformation is working for everyone. I donate a third to the refugees and a third to survivors of the hurricane. I sleep well at night."

"You do. Your dreams?"

"Back to the usual work nightmares of a service industry veteran. Quite refreshing. Amusing even."

"An entire troupe of thespians came thru, without their leader, demanding room and board. They claimed to have been invited by you. What was I to do? I asked about you and they pulled thumbs across their throats, yes, very dramatic. Your phone was dead. What was I to think? They held a wake for you. I attended your wake and gave them several fine bottles of scotch."

"Absurd. Really. You expect reimbursement I imagine?"

Jameson frowned and shook his hands, "No no, I'm over it. So what next? Things are really moving along, ay! Lots of work left to do."

"Well if you attend the regional meeting you may find out. All oppression in the world was not erased with the fall of the old guard. The Geo-engineering conflicts continue, diplomacy is in action. Starblaze Sturgeon has been chosen to speak for the Two Spirited refugees from the South, many will be arriving."

"More Two Spirit people." Jameson said, "Good, I like there being more of us."

"Many and diverse refugees. We must welcome them and make room. Each one could be the last of their people. The world is shrinking and we find ourselves huddled on this island of an ecosystem. There must be an excess of compassion and love in such proximity."

"Okay. I'm with you. That's good for business too. Send the ones that can't fit in here over to my block. I've been hoping for something to get shook up around here for awhile now. There's plenty of room to expand the gardens."

Duffy rolled back under the robo cook while Jameson stood in the kitchen leaning against the wall and recounting the many dramas that occurred in Duffy's absence. Duffy finished the repair and rolled back out, closed the cover and stood up to run the machine. The robo cook sprang to life and like magic the dining room door opened and Louis walked in.

"Welcome." Duffy said smiling, "What can I get for you? Something more than a fresh carrot this time?"

Louis stood in the middle of the dining room, taking in the sights, "It has been a far journey since the authorities chased me out of here."

"I recommend the vegan Poutine." Jameson said, "So good."

"Add jalapenos," Louis said, "and some of that famous Peppermint Hibiscus Ginger Sun Tea. Thank you."

Duffy touched the robo chef in his palm and the three of them gathered at a table in the dining room.

"Starblaze is expected here soon, and the former crew of the Merry Gentleman, those who survived." Duffy nodded, "Perhaps even the troupe."

"We'll be singing sea shanties in a spontaneous musical before the night is done." Jameson said.

"If we're lucky." Duffy stood up and pulled an old stringed instrument from the wall and struck a chord, "The subject of tonight's meeting is women's participation in the new government. Do you imagine you have anything to contribute?"

Jameson paused, "Perhaps not. Isn't the new grand council nearly half women? What's the issue?"

"If you attend, your question may be answered." Duffy said.

"Where is bitter old Duffy who cared nothing for political activism?" Jameson turned and looked over his shoulder, "Your walkabout in the North lands has changed you. In my younger days I would have said not for the better, but I think you are doing the right thing. So I say to you, keep up the good work."

"Thank you for sharing the burden. Shall I set a place for you?"

"Oh no. I offer my thumbs up, but I am in retirement from all politics. A mental health break. I've a birthday bonfire to attend down on the shore, I will sit and drink and watch the stars in the cloudless sky."

"Well then, I return the sentiment: keep up the good work."

Jameson arose and embraced Duffy, "Welcome back Duffy, we missed you."

"Jameson. I love you."

Jameson smiled and gripped Duffy's shoulder as tho remembering something he had forgotten long ago.

Jameson walked towards the front door, and Duffy called out, "If you don't stay up all night perhaps you might like to do some gardening tomorrow morning."

"Late season radishes and greens?" with his hand on the door Jameson pointed at Duffy, "Oh yeah. I have some good seeds."

"I may see them in my dreams then. Happy stargazing Jameson."

After the door closed Louis turned to Duffy, "He seems like a good friend to have."

"I imagine I am fortunate, but sometimes I have my suspicions."

Duffy sat at the table with Louis, "Tell me. What were you really doing on that bridge when the train was stopped?"

Louis leaned back in his chair and laughed so loud that a group of people walking by entered the cafe and finding only two quiet people they became confused and asked where the party was.

"Alright then." Duffy said and reached behind a bookshelf to produce an old black cello and bow string, "It's the cello for you Louis."

Duffy began to play a melody that may have been two centuries old, or perhaps improvised in the dining room of the Far North Cafe that very moment, or from a wave particle duality event happening simultaneously on another world.

43

Pagnellopy held Xippix's arm as they slowly walked out of the hospital and into the light of three suns. One setting, one at three o'clock, and one at sixteen o'clock. A chilly wind blew from a long line of dark clouds on the horizon as fabulous sunset colors streaked in all directions.

"Thanks for borrowing this quadram, I guess I was over confident about being able to walk this far."

Pagnellopy loaded turtle friend into the passenger seat and strapped the safeties, closed the door, and got behind the buttons.

"You want to see Hank first?"

At the sound of his name Hank the Dog jumped from the back seat to the front and licked Xippix's neck.

"Ooooo! Oh! It hurts when I get excited." Xippix said, "Sit in my lap, Hank. Okay. Oookay."

They laughed and motored away in the electric quadram.

"Do we have a lock on government functions, or what? What's the word?" Xippix shook their head, "I don't want to think I suffered bodily harm for nothing. Nightmare factory! I just wanna go back to school and walk my dog in the woods."

"Well, all we gotta do is train some youth to deal with maintaining the environment and our generation will be set up to relax and retire."

"So there will be no relaxing."

"We have a lot more than school bullies to face now. Full grown versions, the council was just the top of the lily pad. These roots go deep. Generational."

"But we have the majority. We have critical mass. Worldwide."

"That doesn't make us any less a target for the minority of haters, no matter how small a percentage they are, they still exist and consolidate power because that's what they live for. Stuck in hate."

Xippix looked out the window as the quadram wound thru the streets of Heart City, toads and turtles talking to each other, holding each other and crying, playing music and dancing with children, digging gardens, swinging cone nets from roof tops, sharing food with their Grandstars.

"We can't live our lives in fear and we cant ignore what our eyes tell us." Pagnellopy said, "When these people emerge we have to confront them, listen to them, and accept that we may never change how they think."

"Just welcome the lot into our community?"

"We must actually open our arms and embrace them. We don't want to hate or destroy people, we want to protect people, we want to protect the planet, right? Those people are part of the planet. You haven't heard about Chartles, have you?"

"What about Chartles?"

"He's in the same hospital you were in. The episode in the forest was a breakout moment for his mental illness. Chartles has gotten help, what he needed years ago, but it takes attempted murder to wake up the caregivers because we all ignore the obvious signs and pretend like nothing is wrong. We have to reach out and ask how people are doing. A lot of people need help. This is our world. One world, many minds, all of them deserve to be heard."

"So Chartles is one of us." Xippix said, "Now that he's gotten help he's probably more stable than we are. I know I have trouble sleeping at night. There's so much to be angry and afraid of."

Pagnellopy steered the quadram in silence thru the crowded central farmer's market of Heart City.

"Stop!" Xippix said, "Hank wants a fish."

Pagnellopy smiled a toad smile and pulled over close to a stall that had many different sizes of dark wooden barrels.

"Wait." Pagnellopy said, "Let me say something, but tell me if this is too much to hear right now. I saw so much of your blood on the outside of your body, Xippix. It had an effect on me." Pagnellopy's head began to glow and toad eyes became dark, "We need help too, don't we?"

Xippix held Pagnellopy's hand, "It's going to get better, because we'll make it that way. We are powerful beings. Look at me, I survived something that I can barely understand and it almost killed me. Now I know how close life is to death, we don't have a moment to loose! The future is right here, in our hands, it always has been, but now I can see it, and I've put my hand in yours and you will put yours in another's and we will encircle the planet and Gaeiou will be a good place to live. The good old days haven't even happened yet! C'mon we're hungry! The hospital serves nothing but green paste."

Pagnellopy jumped out of the quadram and helped Xippix to the snack stand, followed close behind by Hank. From the twilight sky large flakes of snow began to fall, swirling around them in the easy breeze.

"Mmmmm" Xippix savored the first bite and gave the rest to Hank, "We better get some of these to go."

"Let's get a bag." Pagnellopy laughed, "There's a lot of people waiting to see you. We can share."

Xippix smiled, "It feels good to be loved."

Hobo Fires by Robert Wildwood

Available as eBook: www.amazon.com

Hobo Fires is a science fiction graphic novel of the new millennium. Journey along with Poenee as she braves the accelerating future riding on robotic freight trains.

Get the first edition of 336 page graphic novel **Hobo Fires** by ordering direct from the author using Paypal, send $12 (shipping included) and your mailing address to:

robertearlwildwood@gmail.com

Robert Wildwood
at Microcosm Publishing:

U n s i n k a b l e
A w e s o m e   F u t u r e
S h u t   U p   &   L o v e   T h e   R a i n
A l i v e   W i t h   V i g o r !

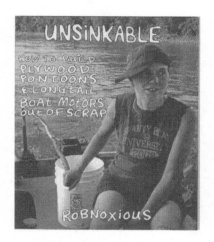

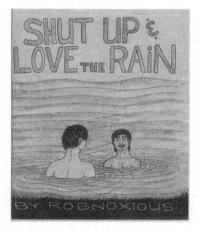

https://microcosmpublishing.com/catalog/artist/robert_wildwood/

Robert Earl Wildwood has published
numerous zines and books under the name Robert
Earl Sutter III, Robnoxious, & Robert Rowboat.

Robert lives in Duluth, Minnesota.

Made in the USA
Charleston, SC
18 August 2016